Bourbons & Bling

Working for Love, Book 5

Amber W. Lynne

Carnelian & Quills

Edited by: Krissy Espindola (KrissyEspindola@gmail.com)
Cover Art by: Rebecca Ruger (BeckandDot@gmail.com)
Paper: ISBN 978-1-960479-33-4
eBook: ISBN 978-1-960479-34-1

For Michile—who has watched every Working for Love book unfold, and whose friendship is woven into every line.

And, to Krissy—who made sure this book made it into the world and into your hands.

Thank you both for sharing the ups, the downs, and all the in-betweens with me.

Chapter One

Ethan

Sunday mornings were not something Ethan Moore had ever really associated with children—particularly when they shared his DNA.

Now, across from him at a bistro table in Central Park sat Rosie Ann Moore—his daughter, who had come from Serenity, Texas, with her mom, Bailey, his ex-wife and current business partner, for spring break.

The wind had tangled her hair into a wild crown. She sipped cocoa, cradling the mug in both hands. "Mr. Ethan, why are you wearing a tie to the park?" She slurped, her boots swinging in a slow-motion assault on the metal chair legs.

Ethan tugged at his tie, wishing he hadn't gone with the purple paisley. "Serious people take their appearance... well, seriously," he said, aiming for authority.

She eyed him over her cup. "You're going to wreck your pants. Mom says no one trusts a grown-up who wears a suit to the park."

Bailey. Of course, no one else would raise a kid who talked like that.... his kid. He reflected in silence, then raised his cup. "Here's to no more suits at the park."

The girl grinned, revealing a missing front tooth that matched the chaotic energy of the fake tattoos running up her arm and the bedraggled pink tutu drooping over her jeans. They were a sight together, with him in his pressed charcoal pants and her in a whirlwind of dirt, tulle, and chaos. Early joggers gave him sympathetic glances.

He ignored them. He hadn't been the best dad to Rosie—he really hadn't been a dad at all—and he was hoping to make that right. Ethan's strategy, if he could call it that, was to let her set the pace. He would prove to Bailey that he deserved more time with his daughter by showing up, even if it meant surrendering his dignity to the whims of a nine-year-old with opinions on mud quality. He'd have to buy a pair of—he shuddered at the thought—jeans for their future adventures.

After breakfast, the plan was to head to the playground. Rosie raced ahead, weaving through puddles and yelping every time she spotted a squirrel. "That one's called Sir Acorns. He's from England!"

Ethan jogged behind her, his coat flapping loosely. He grew winded embarrassingly fast. This was nothing like boardroom bargaining.

"Watch me!" Rosie shouted, already scrambling up the jungle gym.

Ethan half-smiled, cringing at the thought of how much he'd lost and realizing, with a jolt, that he had a long way to catch up. He'd never done the boyfriend, husband, or dad thing right, not with Bailey, or anyone else.

She hung upside down, arms swinging. "How many monkeys, Mr. Ethan?"

He ticked each squealing swing on his fingers. "Five monkeys."

Rosie squinted. "You're supposed to say two! You and me!"

He almost laughed. "Then two monkeys, one for each of us."

She beamed, and he gave in to the rare, unguarded feeling in his chest. This was better than closing any deal. The easy joy on her face was an instant reward.

His phone buzzed in his pocket. He let Rosie finish dismounting the monkey bars before glancing down and squinting at an unfamiliar Seattle area code. There was only one person who would be calling him from the Emerald City.

He answered, voice cautious. "Moore."

Nothing at first. Then a shallow breath. "Ethan?"

He knew that voice, even roughened by pain and distance. "Rowan?"

"Sorry. I—" A hitch, more breathless now. "I'm at the hospital. Seattle General. They think it's my gallbladder. They said something about a surgery tonight, and I can barely think straight."

"Where's Tiffany?"

"She's at my friend Kim's—" Her voice broke with a gasp.

He straightened, old nerves rising. Rosie was dragging a stick in the gravel, blonde head glittering in the rare city sun.

"Is it bad?"

"I don't know." Rowan's voice cracked, raw with fear she

was trying to hide. "They said it's a 'complicated case.' I just—I need you, Ethan. Tiff needs you."

"I'll come. I'll get the next flight out." Something inside him jolted.

"Okay." A faint wince in her tone, like she hated needing anything from him. "I'd like Tiffany to stay in her own home. She loves Kim's kids, and it's just next door, but it's not the same."

"I agree. Tiffany should be in her own home." The relief in her silence made him bite back everything else he wanted to ask. "Text me Kim's number. I'll talk to her."

"Thank you," she whispered.

When the call ended, Ethan bent to Rosie's level, aware of the thunder cloud in his own expression. "Hey, Rosie, change of plans."

She eyed him, always too sharp. "You look scared."

He kneeled further, steadying his breath. "I need to go to Seattle for a few days. We're going to need to get you back to your Mom sooner than planned. I'll call every night until we can see each other again."

Rosie pressed her sticky palm to his. "Is it my sister?"

He nearly coughed. Leave it to Bailey's kid to be direct. "Sort of, it's her mom, Rowan. Tiffany is okay. I need to go see her now."

"Okay. You should help her. That's what dads do."

Ethan looked at his daughter and realized just how damned lucky he was that Bailey was giving him another chance to be the dad he always should have been. "I had fun today. I'm sorry it ended early."

"Me, too. Tiffany needs you, though. I don't mind sharing you. I just wish—"

"I know…" Ethan filled in the pause. "It sucks that we all live so far apart."

"Mom says not to say 'sucks,' but she's not here." Rosie paused and looked around before saying, "It does suck."

"We'll keep working to make that better." Ethan glanced at his phone when a text came through. Kim's number. "I don't know how long I'll be out in Seattle, but maybe we can plan for you to visit there, if it's ok with your mom, so you two can be together while I'm there."

"I'd like that…dad." Rosie nodded, looking as solemn as a kid in a bedraggled tutu can look. "You should bring her chocolate. I think that helps when you're sad."

He ruffled her hair; it was muddy and irrational at the edges. "You're smart, kid."

"I know," she said, grinning.

He took Rosie back to the hotel where she and Bailey were staying, explaining as much as he could. Bailey looked at him, arms crossed, a question in every hard line of her face, but she didn't stop him. "Don't screw it up," she said as he turned to leave, her warning more protective than a threat.

He watched Rosie and Bailey wave from the lobby entrance, sunlight glinting on their joined hands, and realized real life never gave you enough warning before it changed everything.

The cab door had barely closed when Ethan pulled out his phone to book a plane ticket west. His hands shook faintly as he typed in his card number, and the flight confirmation arrived just as the taxi cab dropped him off in front of his apartment to pack his bags.

Thirty-four thousand feet above ground, Ethan pressed his forehead to the cold airplane window. The overhead track lighting painted everything in a tired blue. Outside the window, dusk knifed across the clouds, creating a line between worlds. He drummed his thumb on the tray table, thinking about the cellophane-wrapped candy in his carry-on bag. It'd been his best guess at an olive branch for a daughter who hardly knew him, and a chance to bring a gift from one sister to another. He'd stood at the terminal kiosk for a full five minutes, paralyzed by indecision, before grabbing the biggest chocolate bar he could find. It hadn't felt right. Not big enough, or simply just not... enough.

Somewhere below, in a quiet stretch of Seattle, his daughter slept in a stranger's house. Tiffany's world had fractured with a single hospital call, her mother's voice thin with pain, her routine shattered by an unfamiliar bed. He pictured her curled tight beneath borrowed blankets, small fingers wrapped around that pink unicorn from last year's Christmas photo—the one whose name completely escaped him.

The admission stung. His LinkedIn profile gleamed with achievements: executive titles, seven-figure deals, and industry awards that impressed everyone except two little girls who deserved daily bedtime calls and a father who didn't need a medical emergency to board a plane. Tiffany wasn't just his second daughter. She was also his second chance to become the father he'd failed to be the first time around.

The last time he'd seen Tiffany in person, she'd hidden behind her mother's legs, glancing up with wary eyes. Until recently, he'd been drifting in and out of the margins of her life at birthday parties or during awkward video calls.

Unlike Rosie, who waded into meetings with new people, fists full of frosting and opinions on everything from ballet to barbecue, Tiffany stayed on the edges—softer-spoken, a little haunted in the corners of her smile. The two girls hadn't even known the other existed until a year ago, when the secrets he shared with Bailey—about her father, his affair with Rowan, and their illegitimate daughter—splashed across the front page of every newspaper in Serenity, resulting in their divorce and his move to New York, leaving him across the country from both his daughters.

Tiffany was only a year younger than Rosie, at eight years old, but Ethan realized how much he'd already missed with her, too. When Bailey gave him a second chance with Rosie, he'd promised himself he'd make room for both his girls when things got simpler, when work allowed.

Now, life was forcing his hand.

He felt the ache of regret for how he had treated both women and his daughters. It was a physical ache, as real as the cardboard-sleeved coffee cooling in his hand. Not once in all his years of plotting strategies and mergers had he figured out the formula for rebuilding trust after a late start.

He wondered how it would feel to walk into the neighbor Kim's place, see Tiffany's small shoulders tense at the sight of him, **and have no** right to ask her for anything except for *another* chance.

Chapter Two

Rowan

Rowan hated hospitals. She hated the echo of heels on over-waxed linoleum floors, the sour bouquet of antiseptic, and the way time evaporated beneath a fluorescent flicker. The metallic taste of panic that had brought her there still lingered on her tongue.

When a sudden white-hot pain, worse than any she'd had before, forced her to double up on the kitchen floor. She'd lain there, pressing her cheek to the cold tiles, stubbornly bargaining with her own body. *It would pass.*

Another twenty minutes had passed before she'd given up and called Kim, her voice trembling as she'd asked, "Can you come over? I need help."

Kim's car had become an ambulance by default, barreling through midday rain and traffic while Rowan clenched the seatbelt in one hand and her phone in the other.

Now, she was slumped in a curtained pre-op bay with an IV taped on her wrist. There'd been a parade of medical staff. Her own voice felt paper-thin from repeating answers: why she was alone, how long it had been since she'd last eaten, what her pain felt like. *Fire.*

To distract herself, she'd focused on counting the leaves in the faded watercolor print hung in a time-etched gold frame on the wall. Twenty-one greens, nine yellows, and two so smudged they looked more like clouds than leaves.

Her breath shivered against the chill that had nothing to do with her temperature. Every beep and shuffle in the ward reminded her that she was supposed to be the one keeping Tiffany's world spinning. There were school lunches, permission slips, and bedtime stories to tell. Rowan couldn't be the mom tethered to a drip, wondering who'd braid her daughter's hair tomorrow.

She tried to muster the usual bravado that being a single parent required, but the effort collapsed as another cramp twisted through her side. Who would call the shots if she took too long to get better? Who'd sit with Tiffany at night, explaining why her mom wasn't home yet?

A nurse bustled in. Her words were brisk, but her hands were gentle. Rowan nodded along, stomach churning, heart pounding as the woman read through the care plan. All she could do was wait, count leaves, try not to cry, and hope—for Tiffany's sake and her own—that everything would be fine.

"Vitals look stable," the nurse said, fiddling with her wrist. "Do you have anyone coming to be with you today?"

Rowan's stomach twisted into knots. "My daughter's with a neighbor. Her...dad is flying in from New York." She still hesitated over the word 'dad,' as if saying it too loudly would jinx something vital. It'd been nearly a decade of doing it all herself. Letting Ethan in, even now, after the gulf between them, felt like balancing on a fraying tightrope.

Since her daughter's birth, she'd handled every sleepover permission slip, stomach bug, and school drop-off solo. Her grip on independence was muscle-deep but worn ragged. Letting Ethan in now, even in a crisis, felt less like relief and more like ceding ground she'd fought hard to hold. Guilt gnawed at her for not being there for Tiffany, for not holding Ethan accountable sooner as a father rather than just a child support provider, and for asking him now, which felt more desperate than deliberate.

The nurse lingered a second, offering a distant, practiced smile. "That's good. No one should have to do this alone."

She was gone before Rowan could attempt an explanation, the curtain closing with a sigh against Rowan's exposed ankle.

Alone again, Rowan shivered despite the heat throbbing beneath her skin. Each pulse in her belly threatened another stab of pain, as if her organs had joined the mutiny. She pressed her palm to the offending spot, counting each ragged breath as her mind spun through possibilities: infection, complications, and what-ifs that stretched beyond the IV line tethering her to this place.

She'd built her life on endurance and iron will.

Many times, over the years, she'd smiled through customer meetings with a cough stitched tight in her chest or hauled herself to conventions and gallery shows while ignoring aches and pains. But tonight her hands wouldn't steady.

Rowan hated, truly hated, how small she felt, wishing for

help and dreading it at the same time. A thousand old arguments surfaced. *It's easier not to need. It's safer not to ask.* But she'd already called Ethan, and she wanted him to come through for Tiffany, really, for both of them.

That want, equal parts hope and fear, left her feeling more exposed than the hospital gown gaping at her back.

Her phone chimed on the bedside tray, and a text previewed across the cracked screen.

Kim: *Tiff is fine. Made her eat pizza while watching a movie. Call us with news.*

Rowan smiled, relief loosening her shoulders an inch. She thumbed out a reply with clumsy hands: *Tell her I love her to the moon and back...and I'll be home as soon as I can.*

A second text popped in. For a moment, she stared at it, skin prickling, waiting for the rush of guilt she'd always felt when Ethan tried to offer help she refused, afraid the price would be her independence...or her pride.

She picked the phone up and read his text.

Ethan: *En route. Flight lands at 6:42 a.m. then I need to rent a car. Will get Tiff as soon as I can. Hang in there.*

Simple. No flourish. No lectures or questions. Somehow, that steadiness calmed her more than the morphine drip currently humming in her arm.

She set the phone aside, breathing easier.

A doctor bustled in, his white coat bright against the blue-walled bay—cheerful but ominous all the same. Rowan shrank deeper into the pillow.

"Ms. Fontaine? I'm Dr. Cole. If you'd like, you can call me Lucas. We spoke earlier about your gallbladder. Labs confirm the infection's advanced. We'd like to operate within the next few hours, give or take, based on operating room availability. Is that alright?"

Rowan nodded, or maybe her chin just dipped, limp with fatigue. "What about after? The recovery?"

Dr. Cole drew a line down his palm with a pen while explaining things in bullet points that Rowan could barely follow. "A few days in the hospital. There could be potential complications given your blood work, but we'll be watching for trouble. Is there anyone you want us to call?"

Out of habit, Rowan wanted to say no, but she laced her hands across her stomach and answered quietly, "My...ex will be here as soon as he can. You can also call my neighbor, Kim, if you need a local contact."

"I'll have the nurse confirm we have their numbers." The doctor nodded, his tone gentle. "We'll keep everyone updated."

He moved methodically through his checklist while Rowan's world narrowed to the scratch of the pen, the rhythm of the IV pump, and the raw ache twisting through her side.

As the door clicked shut behind the doctor, Rowan pressed her face to the edge of the starched pillow. No matter how hard she squeezed her eyes shut, she couldn't hold herself together. The walls she kept razor-straight in daylight crumbled under the dim fluorescent lights and the press of solitude.

Anger—her usual shield—wouldn't come. What rose instead was quieter and more humiliating: the wish that someone might care enough to sit at her bedside and tell her everything would be all right, and that it wasn't all on her, not tonight.

She didn't want to need Ethan. She'd built her life around

not needing him—threading independence into every decision—even when it meant keeping Tiffany at arm's length from the father who, for so long, hadn't bothered to claim more.

Asking for help still tasted like failure. The shame of it burned in her chest, stubborn and hot. She scrolled their message history, rereading the most recent texts until the words blurred.

The hospital room tilted toward dusk. A soft buzz broke the hush—a photo flashing onto the screen. Ethan, somewhere over the Midwest, with a rocky streaked skyline framed in a plane window behind him.

Ethan: *Landing in a few hours. Tell Tiffany I'll be there around breakfast.*

Rowan: *Okay, she's going to need a ride to school.*

The three dots blinked on her screen long enough to make her uncomfortable.

Rowan: *Kim has the details.*

Ethan: *I'll figure it out.*

Rowan tucked the phone to her chest, trying to steady her breath. Was it cowardice to have called him? The fear of waking up in pain, with no hand to hold, needled at her resolve. But, this wasn't only about her. What if something went wrong? Worse, what if she didn't wake up at all?

"Stop catastrophizing," she whispered into the quiet room, before typing a quick note to Kim to check on Tiffany, and fussing with the pain pump until her thumb ached.

Her mind fought sleep, rehashing every prickly word, every missed birthday, every time she'd told herself Tiffany didn't need Ethan as long as she stayed strong. Now, forced flat on her back, strength was a lie and pride a brittle, useless thing.

When she finally drifted off, her dreams flickered. There was a slice of late sun through cotton drapes, the ghost of a small hand pressed into her palm, and, faint in her awareness, the hope that when morning came, everything would change.

Chapter Three

Ethan

The in-car navigation guided Ethan to a small parking lot next to a neat row of townhouses tucked behind a tangle of maple trees. The damp Seattle morning bit through his suit jacket, cool enough to make him wish he hadn't ditched his tie somewhere over Montana. He'd rolled his sleeves up in the airport bathroom, and with every mile between him and New York, he seemed to come a little more undone.

Following the signs, he found the unit number Kim had texted him. The porch smelled faintly of wet cedar, and a hint of detergent wafted from a nearby dryer vent. A kid's chalk drawing—a unicorn with lopsided wings—was etched across the concrete sidewalk.

He balanced a paper grocery sack with one arm and knocked.

The door opened, revealing a woman in leggings and a soft pink sweatshirt that read 'Coffee First' across the front. Her brown hair was piled into a messy knot, and her gaze was sharp.

"Ethan?" She looked him up and down. "You look like you haven't slept."

"Accurate," he said. "Kim?"

"That's me." She tipped her chin toward the living room as she stepped back. "Tiffany is on the couch. She woke up early to watch cartoons. She's holding up, but I'm sure she'll feel better once she's back in her own home."

"Thanks for taking her." His throat tightened. "I know her mom appreciates the help."

"Don't thank me. Rowan takes my kid when I'm on call." Her tone softened. "We owe each other forever."

Her place was clean and cozy, all soft throws and framed finger paintings. On the couch, a little girl sat cross-legged, wrapped in a star blanket, eyes on a cartoon fish wearing a football helmet, making questionable decisions. Red-gold hair fell in a messy swing across her cheek. When she heard his shoes, her shoulders twitched tight, then settled. She looked over and met his gaze dead-on.

"Hi," she said, voice small and stubborn at once.

"Hi, Tiffany." He put the grocery sack on the coffee table. "I brought...breakfast." He fished out a loaf of bread, a jar of peanut butter, a banana, and, because he'd panicked in the aisle, dinosaur gummy vitamins.

Her mouth quirked. "Those are not breakfast," she said, pointing at the dinos.

"I'm aware." He lifted the banana. "This is breakfast."

She slid out from under the blanket, toes peeking from mismatched socks, and padded to the table. Up close, she had a sprinkle of freckles and the same wary eyes from the Christmas photo he'd stared at on his phone while flying West.

"Mom says protein first," she said, peering at the food laid out on the table next to the bag. "And bananas are nature's candy,' but only if they have spots."

He held up the banana. "This one's halfway to spotted?"

"Passable," she decided. "We can make a peanut butter banana sandwich."

Ethan was struck by equal parts horror at the idea and relief that he'd passed his first 'dad' test.

At the door, Kim snagged a spare key from a ceramic dish and pressed it into Ethan's palm. "For Rowan's place. Bring it back when you get one of your own."

"Thank you," he said, pocketing it and refilling the paper bag of groceries before lifting it onto his hip.

Tiffany slipped on her backpack without being asked, and he followed her out. The walk was only half a block—past Kim's blue and violet blooming hydrangeas and up the short path to a second townhome with the teal-painted door Rowan had once posted on Instagram with the caption: *#ChaseJoy*.

Ethan fit the key into the lock. It turned with a soft click.

Inside, the air was faintly musty, threaded with the sour trace of old food. He quickly took in the small space. There was a corner filled with toys, a table by the door covered in envelopes, and a half-finished necklace rested on a tray by the couch, its beads arranged in careful, patient rows.

Tiffany kicked off her shoes and hovered beside the couch.

"Want me to see if I can find that cartoon you were watching?" he asked.

She nodded, small and serious.

He found the remote buried under a throw pillow and hit the power button, then flipped through channels until her show filled the screen. Tiffany curled into the corner of the couch, knees tucked tight, eyes fixed on the opening theme like it was a lifeline.

"Alright, breakfast," he said, heading for the kitchen. "Where are the plates? A Knife?" He randomly checked cabinets and drawers. *Victory.* He twisted off the lid of the peanut butter jar and peeled back the foil. "Slices or mash on the banana?"

"Slices. Coins. Not too thin or they just get mooshy anyway."

"Got it. Banana coins." He cut thick rounds, spread peanut butter, and glanced over. "Honey? Yes or no?"

"Yes," came from the couch. "Sometimes Mom does that, too."

He grinned and used the back of the spoon to make a thin amber zigzag of nutty paste. "Crusts?"

"That's where the nutrients are." She tore her gaze from the screen, weighing his question as it mattered. "Cut diagonally. Triangles taste better."

"Science." He pressed the halves, made the cut, and set the plate on the coffee table with a glass of milk. "Okay, eat up. I have to figure out how to get you to school soon."

She chewed, relaxed by degrees, and pointed at the napkins. He handed one over, glanced at the clock on the stove, and did the quick math to make the 8:45 a.m. drop off.

Tiffany was quiet at first, watching him out of the corner of her eye. He sat on the floor at her level, half on his heels.

She watched as the cartoon fish on the show made another ridiculous decision.

Tiffany snorted. "I do not approve of his choices," she said.

"Me either." He peeled a banana, his hands clumsy, and took a bite. "Anything big we have to plan for today?"

She shrugged, chewing. "It's Monday. We do spelling, and then we go to the library." A pause. "Mom always makes me bring the books back on time even if I'm not done with them, yet."

"That's hard, but important. I try to do that, too," he said. "Mostly."

"Mom says you're a businessman," she said, cautious but curious, testing a little.

He felt all his old defenses line up, then let them fall. "I am, but not while I'm here. Right now, we're going to focus on taking you to school, and then I'm going to go see your mom when she wakes up."

Tiffany's chin tipped—a subtle reach for control that Rowan had likely taught her when life didn't give a lot of choices. "Is she okay?"

"She's having surgery, but she wanted you taken care of, too. The doctors are focused on doing their jobs so she can come home." He forced his voice to steady. "Before she went into surgery this morning, she made me promise to tell you she loves you to the moon and back."

Tiffany's fingers tightened around her sandwich, and a chunk of banana slipped out. "She says that a lot."

"It's true a lot," Ethan said.

He got up and started rummaging through the cabinets,

trying to cobble together a lunch before wondering whether it would be easier to buy one at her school. He finished unpacking the groceries from the paper bag and held up the bottle of dinosaur vitamins. "Think these'll make us stronger?"

Tiffany swallowed hard, then walked over and nudged the vitamins toward him. "Maybe. You can take one, too."

He didn't laugh. He didn't shrug it off. He just opened the stupid childproof cap and swallowed a green T-Rex that tasted like sugar and regret. "Officially strong," he said. Her smile flashed and then disappeared.

She held out her hand, and he dropped a red stegosaurus into her small palm before she popped it in her mouth. "Now, we're prepared to get ready."

Tiffany disappeared into the bathroom to brush her teeth for "two songs," and he started loading her backpack: lunchbox, water bottle, a library book with a fox on the cover, and a crumpled permission slip that looked like it had been home more than once.

He held it up. "Should this go back today?"

"Field trip," she said, mouth full of toothpaste foam. "To the tide pools in two weeks." A blush crept up her neck. "Mom said she'd try to go, but then she...got sick." The word landed heavily.

Ethan scanned the slip. Boxes were unchecked. Parent signature line blank. He felt the familiar itch to outsource, to call an assistant, to pay someone to make this not a problem, but there was nobody to call. He found a pen in the kitchen junk drawer—half-dead, chewed cap—then he signed in a loopy signature that had finalized more than one contract.

He stared at the form for a moment before he asked, "Can I?" He pointed to the chaperone line. "If your teacher says yes."

Tiffany stared at the empty line. Then she nodded fast, a little too fast, as if she didn't want to give him time to change his mind. "Okay."

She disappeared into her room and emerged in leggings with tiny stars and a blue sweater, a shade too big. He reached for the zipper of her jacket and paused, waiting. She tipped her chin up. He zipped slowly, careful to avoid hair and skin.

He crouched to meet her eyes. "Ready?"

"Ready," she echoed. Then, in a quieter voice, she asked, "Are we going to be late?"

"We're going to be perfectly on time." He didn't even know if that was true, but he wasn't ready to start the day by letting down an eight-year-old.

The gray Seattle morning brightened as they slid into traffic. Rain freckled the windshield. Tiffany had buckled herself in and stared out the window, humming under her breath.

He cleared his throat. "We can go see your mom after school. Then we can bring her something...but not flowers," he added, because he already knew that hospitals had opinions about pollen and glitter.

"Books," Tiffany said wisely. "She likes mysteries, but not with scary men, or dumb ladies."

"Strong, smart women only. Got it." He turned into the school lot and immediately realized he had entered a world with rules no one had posted. SUVs idled in intricate choreography. Children poured from doors in rows, and parents in puffer jackets hurried along the sidewalk.

Tiffany's hand snuck out and found his sleeve, not quite holding on, but definitely anchoring.

Inside, the school smelled of pencil shavings and the faint musk of damp coats and wet sneakers.

He followed the river of small bodies down the hall, Tiffany half a step at his side, tugging him forward through the current toward the office.

Once they stepped inside the glass-walled room, the hallway noise softened to a low, muffled hum. The secretary—silver bob, glasses on a beaded chain—looked up and smiled with the crisp kindness of a woman who could run an army.

"Good morning." Her gaze flicked over Ethan, then settled. "You must be Mr. Moore. Rowan called."

"Ethan." He exhaled. "Yes. Hello."

Tiffany stood taller for the introduction. "He's my Dad."

Unaware of how much that meant to the little girl, the woman smiled and introduced herself. "I'm Marcy," she said. "We've got Tiffany all set for you. Her teacher knows the plan. Here's a visitor badge for pick-ups this week." She slid a small slip of thick paper across the counter. "And this is our 'How To' sheet."

"I hope it gives instructions for navigating the car-mageddon out front."

"It does," she said, with a wink and a faint look of empathy.

Ethan took the sheet and nodded like she'd presented him with a boardroom brief on exit strategies. "Thank you."

A pair of moms swung through the doorway with a tray of coffees and plenty of curious looks. One smiled brightly at him. "Oh, are you Tiffany's dad? We haven't seen you at pickup," she said, her voice dripping charm.

Ethan didn't flinch. "New in town," he said lightly.

Marcy got his attention again with a pointed tap on the counter. "Tiffany, honey, your teacher asked for your homework packet. The one with the purple cover?"

Tiffany's eyes darted to Ethan. He rifled through the backpack. No purple. He scanned his morning timeline, panic hunting for places he could rewind. Kim's front table. The pile by the door. The junk drawer. *Purple, purple, purple...*

"The front door," Tiffany muttered, dismayed. "I put it by my shoes so I wouldn't forget."

He could feel her bracing for disappointment. He shook his head. "It's okay. I'll bring it after school," he said, making a note on the internal list that usually held numbers and percentages, but now held a child's priorities. "Tell your teacher that's on me."

Marcy looked like she wanted to hug him. "You got this," she murmured, too low for the peanut gallery.

Tiffany's mouth softened, but anxiety still rang under her skin. "Will you...be here at two forty-five?" She asked, and he heard everything riding on the question.

"Better, I'll be here at two-thirty," he said. "You won't miss me."

She studied his face. Then, without warning, she threw her arms around his ribs in a brief, fierce hug. He didn't have time to think. He hugged back, one hand firm between her shoulder blades.

She peeled away fast, cheeks pink. "Okay," she said and nodded before she reassured herself one more time. "Okay."

The office buzz settled around him. Marcy's voice cut in, gentle but brisk. "You're doing better than most," she said, as if he'd asked. She slid a tiny neon post-it note towards him. "This has the nurse's line, my line, and the attendance line. There's also the PTA Facebook group, which is like feeding time at the shark tank, but with bake sales."

He huffed a laugh. "I owe you something stronger than coffee."

"You can repay me by bringing back Tiffany's homework and making sure she stays safe while her mom heals," she said. Then her voice softened, not for show. "And by being on time at two forty-five."

"I will be here," he said, and meant it with a ferocity that surprised him.

Outside, the air tasted like rain. He sat in the car with both hands on the steering wheel and let out a breath he hadn't realized he'd trapped in his body since New York.

His phone buzzed with a text from an unknown number: *This is Dr. Cole. Rowan's recovering in post-op and should be back in her room soon. We'll keep sending updates.*

He typed fast, thumbs clumsy: *Thank you. I'll be there as soon as I can.*

Then another message lit the screen.

Kim: *How'd it go?*

He snapped a quick photo of the visitor badge clipped to his jacket and hit send.

Then, with only the slightest hesitation, he opened a new text to Rowan.

Ethan: *Maybe you'll see this before you see me. Drop-off complete. She's brave. I forgot the purple homework packet. Will report back.*

He closed his eyes and rested his head against the seat. The day stretched in front of him—hospital waiting rooms, two-thirty hard stop, dinner that needed to be 'healthy' and kid-friendly. He was out of his depth. He was also, for a change, exactly where he was supposed to be.

Ethan put the car in gear and pulled onto the road. This was Seattle. There had to be coffee strong enough to make sense of all this somewhere nearby.

Chapter Four

Rowan

Rowan surfaced through cotton-thick sleep to the steady beep of a monitor and the ache that curled like a dull fist under her ribs. Her mouth felt like she'd licked an old envelope. The room was half-shadowed, blinds tilted to dull the morning. Someone had tucked the blanket tight around her hips. The IV tugged at her wrist when she shifted.

The scent hit her next—coffee, real and dark, cut with a hint of cardamom from some long-ago perfume that had soaked into her hoodie. No, not hers. The navy sweatshirt draped over the back of the visitor chair was too neat to be hers. Ethan sat in that chair, legs long, chin dipped to his chest, the cup balanced in his palm. He'd lost the jacket. The roll of his sleeves rested at his forearms. The line of his throat was unguarded in the thin hospital light.

She tried to swallow, failed, and made a small sound that betrayed her. Ethan lifted his head fast, green eyes sharp and awake. Perhaps he hadn't been sleeping at all.

"Hey," he said, voice low. "You're back."

"Feels debatable," she rasped.

He stood, the chair legs scuffing the linoleum, then eased a straw to her lips before she could fight him. Water tasted like nectar. He watched her sip, careful. When she leaned away, he set the cup down and held up the coffee with an apologetic lift of his brow. "Contraband, cleared by Nurse Kelly," he said.

"I never pegged you for a rule follower."

"I'm a fast learner when a nurse glares at me."

The corner of her mouth tugged. "Just a sip?"

He glanced towards the door, then edged the lid back and offered her the tiniest sip. Heat slid over her tongue, bitter and honest. She let it sit under her tongue, then swallowed and breathed around the ache in her belly.

"What time is it?" she asked.

"Ten-thirty," he said, glancing at the clock. "They said you'd be in and out for a bit."

"How long have you been here?"

He hesitated like he was doing math, but didn't want her to know. "A little after school drop off."

She blinked up at him. "Did you...go home?"

"I went to the townhouse to grab my laptop and almost died of a heart attack when your cat decided to emerge. It was hiding like it's in witness protection. Then I came here."

"Fig," she murmured. "She likes people best when they feed her tuna."

He smiled at that, quick and quiet, then reached for the blanket and smoothed the corner where she'd bunched it. His fingers brushed the back of her hand, a light pass that left warmth behind.

"Don't hover," she said, though the words lacked bite.

"You always were too independent," he said, but his hands remained resting on the bed. "How do you feel?"

"Like someone replaced my insides with gravel." She shifted and winced. "Also, like I lost a fight with a stapler."

His gaze slid to the small bandage beneath the hospital gown tie. His frown conveyed a desire to fix what was beyond repair. "They said the surgeon is happy," he offered. "Infectious disease is watching you, which sounds dramatic, but your labs are better."

"You understood all that?"

"I Googled it this morning," he said, sheepish but not ashamed. "I also had Nurse Kelly explain it to me like I was six."

Rowan laughed and regretted it, a sharp stitch tugging deep. He saw the flash across her face and steadied the bed rail with one hand, as if that could help. "Easy."

"I hate this," she said, the words spilling out before pride could catch them. "Not the pain, though that's a treat. Being stuck. Tiff being scared. People looking at me like I'm—"

"Breakable?" he supplied.

"Useless," she corrected. "And yes. Breakable, too." She stared past him at the strip of sky between the blinds, a thin blade of white-gray Northwest morning. "I'm supposed to be the one who keeps us held together."

"You still are," he said, not rushing it, not filling the air with talk. "Keeping things going doesn't always have to be doing everything yourself."

Her throat went tight. "That's a nice sentence for a motivational poster."

"Fine. Here's a less pretty version," he said.

He pulled the visitor chair closer, sat, and dragged the trash can with his foot so the IV line had room. He placed his forearms on the bed's edge. "You scared me, and I don't like being scared. When I'm scared, I control whatever I can. So I'm here with coffee, and I learned the nurse's names, and, when it's time, I'll set alarms on my phone for your meds like a one-man pharmacy. And I'm taking our kid to school on time, even if I forget the purple packet before I even knew we needed it."

The word *our* wasn't casual.

She looked down at their hands, where they rested inches apart on the sheet. Her fingers twitched, and he met her halfway without making it a thing, his hand sliding over hers, warm and steady, an apology disguised as a touch. He didn't squeeze. He didn't pat. He was there, thumb resting at the base of her knuckles, the warmth of him sinking through into skin and bone.

"You're not useless," he said. "You're post-op and exhausted and mean when you're hungry, which I respect. I will defend you against bland pudding with my life."

Her laugh came out like a hiccup. "Please do. If they bring me one more cup of broth, I might attempt an escape."

"Duly noted." He lifted the coffee again. "Two sips? Or I can be sneaky and drink it myself and lie."

"Two sips."

She took them, then leaned back, eyelids heavy. Fatigue rolled through her. She fought it because she had fought everything for so long, and because this—him by her side, their daughter's world still turning—felt precarious and precious. "How was Tiff this morning?"

"Quiet until she wasn't," he said, a trace of fondness softening his tone. "She wore the sweater with stars and made sure I knew the perfect way to cut a banana. She's...okay."

Rowan's eyes burned. "She's brave when she has to be," she whispered.

"Wonder where she gets that."

"I wish she didn't have to—"

The door clicked open, and a nurse swept in wearing navy scrubs patterned with tiny foxes.

"Kelly." Ethan greeted her as he stood up to make more room around the bed. "Hello."

"How's the pain?" Kelly asked, eyes tracking the monitor while deftly maneuvering the blood pressure cuff around Rowan's arm.

"Manageable, it's going to be a while before I try to join a Zumba class," Rowan said, wincing as the cuff tightened. "Mostly tired."

"Good. Your fever's down. We like that. We're keeping you on antibiotics." Kelly glanced up at Ethan. "I see you're keeping your coffee to yourself."

"Absolutely," he said, straight-faced, but hoping she couldn't smell the few small sips on Rowan's breath.

"Keep the sass," she said, amused. "It helps around here. I'm going to check your incision, Rowan." She turned to Ethan. "Step outside for two minutes? Then you can rush back in and fuss convincingly."

"On brand," he said, and stood. He paused long enough to

slide his palm from Rowan's to the sheet like a promise and then slipped out into the hallway.

Kelly lifted the gown edge with brisk care. "Looks clean. Little bruising, nothing that worries me," she said, more to Rowan's creeping anxiety than to the chart. "Your body's had a rough week, hun. Let it have today to rest."

"I hate asking for help."

"Most of my favorite people do," Kelly said, snapping the gown tie back into place. "Let him help."

"He's...different," Rowan said, surprising herself. The room went soft around that truth. "Present.""Good word." Kelly tossed her a conspirator's smile and wheeled the vitals cart toward the door. "Alright, nap while you can. I'll be back to poke you more later."She left the door half-open.

Ethan came back and approached the bed slowly, clearly checking on her without asking. He lowered himself into the chair again. The space between them was filled with a quiet that said more than either of them could.

"I'm supposed to walk this afternoon," she said, her eyelids lowering. "They're big on getting laps.""I'll be here," he said. "I can even go grab some sneakers." He winced, then smiled."Wow. You'd give up your loafers for me?""Anything that helps you get better."

Her smile came slowly. The steady heat of his skin settled her, the way a palm pressed to a fevered forehead settles a child. She let her eyes close.

"Ethan?""Yeah.""Thank you," she said, the words shaped by sincerity instead of pride. "Not for the coffee, but for not making me ask twice.""You called. I came."

Her throat tightened, a tender ache that had nothing to do with stitches. Sleep tugged at her. The world narrowed to the beeps, the slide of his thumb at her knuckle, the memory of Tiffany's smile.

"Thank you for taking care of my girl.""Our girl," he said, quiet but sure. "You don't have to do this alone. If Nurse Kelly clears it, she'd love to see you."

Rowan sank deeper into the pillow and grimaced. "Not like this. Maybe after I've proved I can do a lap, or two."He nodded. "Then we'll video call tonight. We'll keep it short and sweet."

He hesitated, just a fraction. "There's...something else I wanted to ask you. I want to be clear, I'm not trying to decide anything without you."

Her eyes opened. "Okay."

"I've been thinking about Tiffany," he said. "She's holding it together, but this is a lot. Rosie's spring break is now, Texas is earlier than here - which is why she and Bailey were in New York before I came out here."

Rowan stayed quiet, listening.

"I wondered if it might make things easier on Tiffany if her sister could come out for a few days," he said. "A week, maybe, if I can convince her mom to let her have a couple extra days off school. Something steady. Something normal. I want to ask Bailey if she'd be open to it...but only if you are, too."

The idea settled slowly. Not sudden. Not sharp. Something warmer.

"She does miss her," Rowan said.

"I think they both feel how strange this still is," he said. "And we haven't really had time...all of us together. Maybe this could be that. Not perfect. Just...something."

Rowan swallowed. "I don't want to confuse her.""I don't either," he said. "That's why I'm asking."

She studied his face—the care in it, the restraint. "I think...I think it could be good. For Tiffany, and maybe for us, too."

Relief loosened his shoulders. "Then I'll see what I can do. I'll frame it as a visit. No pressure. No expectations. And, I won't say anything to Tiffany until we know what's happening for sure."Rowan nodded. "Thank you. For doing it that way."

A soft knock, and Kelly breezed in. "Break's over, you two. Vitals, then a nap, and you don't argue." She checked Rowan's lines with brisk care, eyes kind. "Your doctor will start his rounds in a few minutes. Then, after your nap, we'll take a stroll in the hallway later. I'll snag you the good walker."

"Deal," Rowan said, because arguing would take more energy than she had.

Nurse Kelly slipped out. Ethan stood, reluctant to let go, and finally eased his hand from hers with a last, steady press.

"I'll check in later. I want to catch Dr. Cole, and then I'll head out to get Tiff." He tipped her a wry smile. "Try not to have too much fun without me."She would have rolled her eyes if it didn't tug. "Bossy.""Charming," he countered. "Now rest."

He closed the curtain around her bed. It sighed shut.

A cup of ice chips sat on the tray beside her. She stared at the place where his hand had warmed her palm until the imprint faded. He had left her, yes—but his leaving came with a return time. The difference was so simple she might have cried over it if she weren't so damned tired.

She closed her eyes. In the low hum of the room, she let

herself sink into the pillow, into her not having to hold every piece all at once. Somewhere in this building, a man with his sleeves rolled up was grilling a doctor and learning the word for the way gas from a laparoscopic surgery could make your shoulder ache during recovery.

Rowan breathed, careful and slow, reining in her though ts.*Her man?* Not yet—but an anxiety-inducing thought all the same.

Chapter Five

Ethan

The first thing Tiffany did when they reached the aquarium was press her face to the thick glass.

Blue light spilled across her freckles as a school of glittering sardines veered like a flock of birds underwater, turning in one bright, fluid sheet. A stingray drifted overhead on the other side of the tunnel, and she gasped—a small, delighted sound swallowed by the echo of the crowd.

"Do you think he can see me?" she asked, palm flat against the curve of the glass.

"If he can see those handprints, he's probably filing a formal complaint with the janitorial staff as we speak," Ethan said, watching the sweep of a gray wing shadow her hair as the stingray glided past again.

When Ethan had met Tiffany at the school gate, he'd known she'd been worrying all day. He'd dropped to a knee, so they were eye to eye. "Your Mom is doing okay," he'd told her. "The doctors just want her to rest today. So we can't see her yet—but we will soon."

Tiffany's fingers worried the strap of her backpack. "Soon-soon? Or grown-up soon?"

"Soon-soon," he said, letting the word carry its promise. "We can even call her tonight."

That loosened something in her shoulders, and she nodded. He stood, took her hand, and steered them toward the car with a plan he'd formed somewhere between the nurse's station and the school bell: *keep her distracted.*

He'd landed on the aquarium.

Now, ocean light rippled across her sweater, and with each tank, the tight knot he'd carried since morning eased a little more. They wove into the crowd beneath the arched glass. The tunnel smelled faintly of salt and someone's cologne. A toddler shrieked two exhibits back, and a docent in a polo shirt pointed out an eel grinning from a crevice.

"Can we visit the touch tanks next?" Tiffany asked.

"Sure, but first I need to mentally prepare to meet a sea cucumber," he said.

At the tide pool exhibit, a teenage volunteer in a mesh vest reminded them about two-finger touches and soft bellies. Tiffany listened solemnly before reaching into the shallow, foaming water to stroke a sea star. Ethan hovered beside her, elbows locked in a stance meant to project competence, but landing somewhere closer to anxious dad.

"Do it," Tiffany said without looking up.

"When a creature is named 'cucumber,' I question the marketing," he said.

"If you're scared of sea cucumbers, how are you going to

chaperone the *real* tide pools?" She side-eyed him. "You signed a school paper saying you were brave."

"No, I signed a paper that said I'm a chaperone. That's Latin for 'man who buys snacks and carries jackets.'"

The volunteer hid a smile. "The sea cucumbers feel like a wet stress ball," she offered.

"Excellent. I'm familiar with those." He rolled up his sleeves and eased two fingers into the cold water.

The first touch was all wrong. The sea cucumber was cooler than he expected and softer, and when it flexed under his hand, his stomach flinched in sympathy.

"Oh my—okay," he said, because he was a grown man and he had an audience of one who was better at this than he was. He kept his fingers there, steady. "He's...squishier than he looks."

Tiffany's grin flashed. "Told you."

"Add that to my list of revelations this week," he said, flicking water from his fingertips back into the pool.

They moved from anemones that curled their tiny fists around Tiffany's touch to the slow creep of a sea star pulling itself along a rock. When they stepped back to watch a crab scuttle sideways, she leaned into his leg without thinking. The contact was light and brief, there and gone like a wave on the sand. He didn't breathe for a beat, not wanting to spook whatever part of her had allowed it.

On the other side of the room, jellyfish drifted in a cylindrical tank like pale lanterns. The low light turned everyone into silhouettes. Tiffany pressed both hands to the glass again.

"They don't have brains," she said, voice hushed as if the jellies could hear. "But they know how to be jellyfish anyway."

"Some days I envy them," he said. "No email."

"No homework," she said. She tilted her head. "Do you think they forget things?"

It was an odd question from a kid, simple yet sharp. Ethan looked at the undulating bells, the slow ballet of translucent bodies pulsing as if the water breathed for them.

"I think they do what they can with what they have," he said, choosing the truth he could hold on to. "They do their best to keep floating."

Tiffany nodded like that answered something she hadn't asked out loud. She watched the jellies for a full minute, then tugged his sleeve.

"I want to see the octopus," she said. "He's clever. He opens jars."

"We'll keep him away from the pantry," Ethan said, and followed her toward the curve of the next hall.

The octopus was hiding in a cave, one intelligent eye regarding them from behind a curtain of rock like an old man in a window shade. Tiffany waited it out, hands clasped, patience stitched across her face. When a sucker slid along the rock, she pointed like she'd spotted a celebrity.

"Hi, sir," she whispered.

They lingered until her stomach made a grumbling complaint loud enough to hear over the tank filters. He glanced at the wall clock. Rowan would be asleep for the next hour if the nurse had anything to do with it. The idea of sitting on that vinyl chair again soothed and sharpened him in equal measure. He touched his phone in his pocket—a nervous tick he'd developed sometime between New York and this new life, where he set mealtime reminders.

"Tacos?" he asked.

Tiffany's eyes widened. "Fish and chips by the water."

"Hypocritical of us, but I'll allow it."

Outside, the June light trembled across the bay in shivers of silver. The breeze smelled like brine and fried something. Ferris wheel cars turned slowly down the pier, bright against the pale sky. They found a walk-up window where a server was handing out fried fish samples and calling out orders over the hiss of oil.

They sat on a bench with a view of the ferries sliding in and out of the bay, gulls tilting like paper planes overhead, the occasional brazen swoop reminding them that ownership of their fries was temporary. Tiffany swung her feet and considered the tartar sauce selection with gravity.

Tiffany took a bite and went still, eyes closing in reverence.

"This is special," she declared after chewing, which earned them a curious glance from a woman nearby.

"We should inform the jellyfish," he said. "They're missing out."

"Jellyfish can't have french fries," she said, and then, like the thought hurt her, added, "Poor jellyfish."

He handed her a napkin. "Tragic."

She took it and said, without looking up, "Thanks, Dad."

The word landed and broke something open in the middle of him. It wasn't thunder. It was a small, ordinary key turning in a sticky lock, and whatever door it opened had been closed so long he hadn't realized how much air was on the other side.

He didn't move. He didn't make the word a big rock in the middle of the path that would trip them both. Instead, he tipped the vinegar onto his fish and went for a bite that gave him a second to find his voice.

"You're welcome," he said, careful, even. The bench pressed steadily against his spine, and the breeze off the water cooled the heat he hadn't known was rising up his neck. He wiped a smear of tartar sauce from her chin with his thumb, the way he'd seen other fathers do for years in doorways and parking lots.

Tiffany blushed the exact pink of the sunset in the distance. She looked down at her lap like she'd dropped something and couldn't decide if it was hers to pick up.

"You can still call me Ethan," he said quietly, because this had to be hers as much as his. "Or you can call me both. I answer to either."

She shrugged one shoulder. Then she leaned, brief and sure, into his side, the weight of her slight. "Okay," she said, and he counted that as permission to breathe again.

He pulled out his phone. "Want to send your mom a picture of us having fun so she knows we're okay?"

Tiffany wiped her hands on her napkin with exaggerated care. "Wait," she said, and tugged him toward the pier rail. "We need the water—and the Ferris wheel."

They lined up with the giant wheel behind them, blue and white cabins marching into the sky. She tucked herself under his arm like she'd been there a hundred times. He took the photo, checked it for sauce stains and ghoulish angles, and took another for insurance.

He sent the best one to Rowan: *We made sure the jellyfish didn't see us eating their friends.*

For a few seconds, the bubbles on his screen pulsed like a

heartbeat.

Then, Rowan typed: *That smile helped. Tell my brave girl I'm so proud of her.*

He lifted the phone so Tiffany could read. She beamed, then sobered. "Tell her the octopus winked at me," she said.

He typed it.

Rowan's reply came faster, a small octopus emoji, a face with heart eyes, and then: *Nurse says nap, then laps. Come by later if Tiffany didn't exhaust you at the aquarium.*

He took that as an order. "I'm going to try to go back and check on your mom this evening," he told Tiffany. "Maybe Kim can keep an eye on you for just a little bit."

Chapter Six

Ethan

After dinner, they wandered the pier. Ethan won a small packet of sour candies from a claw machine that looked rigged. Tiffany fed a quarter into the slot of a brass telescope and watched ferries ghost across the bay, the beach on Alki in the distance.

"Do you like it here?" she asked, still peering through the lens.

"Seattle?"

"Being here," she said, and the way she said here meant more than the damp wood under their feet.

He stepped closer to the rail and hooked a finger in the curve so he didn't have to decide what to do with his hands. "I like fish that look like they're made of glass. I like eating fish and chips with silly seagulls." He paused. "And I like being with you."

She lowered the telescope and looked at him full-on. "Okay," she said. "Good."

It shouldn't have choked him up, a small okay in a small

conversation. It did anyway.

He wanted to tell her about Rosie, but he still needed to talk to Bailey. He'd used time zones as an excuse, but he knew the sooner he asked, the sooner Rosie might visit.

They looped back through the aquarium for one last pass at the touch tanks, or, as Rosie insisted, "to check on the cucumber."

While Tiffany carefully said goodbye to each sea creature in turn, he pulled out his phone. He stared at the screen as if it might explode and typed out a text he'd been writing in his head all day:

Bailey, I owe you, and I can't send it with Venmo. I'm sorry for what I did and didn't do when Rosie was little. I need to ask you something.

He deleted half, rewrote, and left the apology unchanged. One look at Tiffany smiling at a sea star gave him the courage he needed to hit send.

Three dots blinked. Stopped. Blinked again. His stomach went weightless until he saw her contact pop up on the screen.

She'd called instead.

"Say it again," Bailey said. No sarcasm. No ice. Just tired and sharp.

"I'm sorry," he said, and kept it simple. "I should've shown up differently. You shouldn't have had to be the only grown-up in the room."

On the other end of the line, he heard the small exhale of someone who's been carrying a bag for too long, set it down by one strap. "Okay," she said after a beat. "Noted. And?"

He exhaled. "I was thinking about Rosie. You know, since

she is on spring break now, and Tiffany's still scared. She asked me twice this morning if I would remember two forty-five like I could fall out of the sky between lunch and pickup. Having Rosie here might...give both girls something that isn't worry and fear. I don't want to make this harder for anyone. If you say no, I'll take it."

There was a heavy pause.

Bailey was quiet long enough for him to hear voices in the background—Mac and Rosie, probably, and the clink of dishes. When she spoke, her voice had softened, but not surrendered. "Is this about Tiffany? Or about you wanting to rewrite your own story?"

"Both," he said, because lying would be easier, but it would make everything worse. "But, I have no desire to put either kid in the middle of that."

"Good," she said. "I'm not flying Rosie across the country to be your penance. She's not a prop."

"Never."

"Is Rowan okay with it?"

"Yes," he said quickly. "We talked about it. She should be home soon. I...wanted to ask you before I mentioned it to the girls."

"That's...thoughtful," Bailey said mildly.

He winced. "I'm trying."

Another beat. He imagined her at her kitchen counter, one hip against the drawer, weighing every angle the way she always had.

"I want Rosie to see her sister," she said. "I want her to have you in her life. You know that."

"I do."

"But I also don't want to set her up for something that feels good for a minute and then goes away."

"That's not what this is," he said. "I'm not passing through. I'm here. We already talked about this."

Bailey didn't answer right away. When she did, her voice had softened. "Rosie talks about Tiffany. She likes that she's little. She likes that she gets to be the big sister."

His throat tightened.

"And she likes Rowan," Bailey added. "She told me she makes pretty jewelry and that she listens."

A quiet, undeserved relief moved through him.

"I trust Rowan," Bailey said. "More than I trust you to know what you're doing, yet."

"That's fair."

"But if Rowan trusts you with Tiffany," Bailey continued, "then you can't be doing everything wrong."

He closed his eyes.

"So," she said. "Yes. I think Rosie would love to come." Bailey exhaled. "I'm guessing we're doing this fast. I'll look into flights and send you the details."

"Thank you."

Bailey snorted. "Be careful. If you mess this up—"

"I won't," he said.

"Good," she said. He heard her shift the phone. "And Ethan?"

"Yeah."

"I'm glad you called," she said. "Finally."

When she hung up, he stood for a moment with the phone

still warm in his hand. Before he could arrange his thoughts, Tiffany appeared at his elbow and tugged his sleeve. She dragged him toward a wall map, stabbing a finger at a glossy photo of a rocky beach.

"This is where my class is going for the tide pools," she said. "Ms. Barlow says you have to watch the waves and the rocks at the same time, and if you turn your back, the ocean will eat your shoes."

"I'll bring spare shoes and a whistle," he said.

"You'll look weird," she said, delighted.

"I set the bar high," he said, thinking of a purple paisley tie and marshmallow cocoa in Central Park.

His phone buzzed. He glanced down—no emergency texts, no work calls he was pretending didn't exist—just a message from an unfamiliar Seattle number.

Mr. Moore—this is Ms. Barlow. I got your volunteer form from Tiffany for chaperoning the tide pool trip. We'd love to have you join us. I'll send the details next week.

He turned the screen toward her. "Permission granted."

Her mouth fell open. She clapped a hand over it as if she could preserve the moment and keep it from leaking out. "You got picked," she said through her fingers.

"Looks like my background check didn't scare them," he said.

She bounced once on her toes, checked herself—remembered where she was, who she was supposed to be—and then bounced again because kids can only hold so much grown-up. "You will have to wear shoes that grip. Not...business shoes."

He glanced down at his loafers, which had already seen

more of Seattle in forty-eight hours than his dress shoes had seen of New York in a month. "That's the second time today someone's told me I need new shoes."

They stopped by the gift shop on the way out because he was a dad now, and that apparently came with duties like saying yes to tiny, overpriced plushies. Tiffany chose an octopus barely bigger than her palm, coral pink with a ridiculous face.

"For Mom," she said. "In case she gets lonely before she can come home."

"Good thinking," he said, handing over his card.

They made it back to the car as the sun was setting on their shoulders. On the drive back, Tiffany nodded off mid-sentence about an octopus escape she'd seen on a video. At a long red light, Ethan looked at her in the rearview mirror—the slack mouth, the lashes stuck together in clumps from salt and mist, the octopus plush tucked under her cheek.

Ethan pulled into the small parking lot by the townhouse. He let the car idle one minute longer than necessary, not because he was avoiding going inside, but because Tiffany looked content and he wanted her to stay that way for one more breath.

The sunset was fading into dusky night when he typed a text to Rowan: *We're home—going to call soon with Tiffany. Then Kim's coming over so I can head your way.*

He reached back and brushed his fingers through the air an inch from Tiffany's hair. "Okay, kiddo," he whispered. "Let's go call your mom so we can get you tucked into bed."

She stirred, eyes blinking toward him, her mouth shaping around a yawn.

"Dad?" she mumbled.

"Yeah," he said.

"I'm gonna tell her you're good at aquariums," she said, and he couldn't help it—he smiled.

Inside, he flipped on the kitchen light and put some water on the stove to warm for tea while Tiffany hauled her spelling list to the table. They ran through a few words—make, page, late—Tiffany adding dramatic groans for every silent e. When the timer on his phone chimed, he propped his cell against a salt shaker and hit the video call button.

Rowan answered on the second ring. The room behind her was dim and cool. She sat in a chair by the window in her blue hospital robe. Her face was still pale, but color had seeped back into her cheeks.

Tiffany scooted closer and held up her homework. "We did all the silent vowel words."

Rowan's throat worked. "Smart girl," she said, fingers smoothing the edge of her robe. Her eyes lifted to Ethan's on the tiny screen. For a heartbeat, it was an entire conversation: *You're getting it right. You're here. Thank you.*

He nodded once—no promises, he hadn't learned how to keep...yet.

A nurse stepped into frame long enough to tap Rowan's shoulder and make the universal wrap-it-up sign. Rowan rolled her eyes toward the ceiling in theatrical suffering, then looked back at the screen.

"Three more minutes," she said. "I wish I could be there

with you guys."

"Me, too," Tiffany agreed. "We're going to read books after this."

"Bring on the bedtime stories," Ethan said.

They signed off with a bedtime screen kiss and a promise to call in the morning. As the call ended, Tiffany pressed her palm to the cool phone face, then slid off her chair.

"Bedtime?" she asked.

"Bedtime," he said.

He read a few pages of a dog-and-bear book while she rubbed the octopus's arm between her fingers like a worry stone. Halfway through the chapter, a soft knock sounded. Kim poked her head in, hair in a bun, eyes kind.

"Relief crew," she said.

He lingered by Tiffany's bed a moment longer. Her damp lashes clumped from her bedtime bath, and she held the octopus tucked beneath her chin.

"Dad?" she murmured, not quite awake.

"Yeah."

"Tell mom about the octopus," she said, in a fading whisper while pushing the plush toy towards him.

"I will," he said.

He thanked Kim, grabbed his keys, and stepped out into the blue of the evening.

In the reflection of the front picture window, he caught a quick glimpse of himself—a man who looked like he belonged where he was.

It filled his thoughts as he got into his rental car and headed for the hospital.

Chapter Seven

Rowan

Evening had settled over the ward in slow phases. Televisions in neighboring rooms glowed on mute, their light flickering across the hallway tiles. The air vents whispered, carrying the clean, chemical scent of disinfectant and, faintly beneath it, something sweet. The murmurs outside faded as the lights dimmed, leaving only the soft beeps of the monitors.

The soft scrape of the curtain and a tug at her blanket pulled Rowan from sleep. Ethan stood at the foot of her bed with a nurse, his palm flattening a corner of the blanket near her feet.

The evening nurse's eyes crinkled. "It's a little late for visitors, Ms. Fontaine, but I'll allow it." She checked Rowan's surgical drain with brisk, practiced hands, then adjusted the IV rate. "Pain?"

"Better when I don't breathe," Rowan said.

"Well, we need you to keep doing that, too." The nurse nodded, satisfied, then rested a hand on the bed rail. "Visiting hours are...flexible until I finish charting." Her smile had a conspirator's edge. "Thirty minutes." Then she was gone, sneakers whispering down the hall.

Ethan set something on the rolling tray. A palm-sized octopus in coral pink blinked up with embroidered eyes.

"Tiffany insisted. She didn't want you to be alone," he said. "His name is Sushi."

Emotion rose in Rowan's throat as quickly as a hiccup. "A little on the nose, huh?"

He took the chair, closer than this afternoon, forearms on the mattress edge. The bedside lamp threw warm light along his jaw. He looked like New York had blunted him and Seattle had done the rest—tie gone, sleeves rolled up, attention focused right here.

"How's she doing?" Rowan asked.

He tipped his head, a smile slipping loose. "Aquarium conquered. Touch tanks explored. We ate fish and chips while the jellies judged us from a distance."

"That sounds like a perfect adventure."

"She was falling asleep halfway through her bedtime story," he said. "Kim's got her. She's promised breakfast that is, per Tiffany, 'actually edible.' You set a high bar with this home-cooked meal thing."

"I don't have the same endless resources as you."

She watched a scowl cross his face, and the ache under her ribs tightened for reasons that had nothing to do with stitches. It wasn't an unfamiliar topic for them. Hoping to save the mood, she changed the subject.

"I'm glad you took her," she said, and the truth of it scraped away her pride.

He watched her for a beat. "You look like you're bracing for me to say the wrong thing."

"I'm bracing for...everything." Her fingers toyed with one soft octopus arm. "I'm tired, Ethan. Not nap-tired. Years-tired." The confession slid out, unvarnished. "Some days I feel like I'm sprinting between forest fires with a thimble full of water."

He didn't tell her how she should be feeling. Instead, he reached across the sheet and covered her hand, careful not to bump any tape or tubing. The weight of his palm steadied her. "You've held more than your share," he said. "Let me hold some."

Her throat tightened. "I don't know how."

"Me either," he said. "But I'm here."

She stared at their hands. "When I found out I was pregnant, you were always on a plane or in a meeting, and I was... terrified. It felt easier to do everything than to ask and risk you saying no. Or worse—that you'd say yes and then not show up."

He winced. "With Bailey, I wrote checks. I thought that counted. I didn't know how to push past polite parental exchanges. I think I talked to her attorney more than I talked to her. I told myself if you needed me, you'd ask."

"I made a religion out of being fine," she said, her mouth tipping without humor. "If I kept my walls up, I didn't have to admit it hurt when you didn't try to climb them."

"I didn't know you wanted me to..."

"I get it. Tiffany wasn't a plan. She was a person."

"We were new, too."

"I told myself you didn't want her. Anger felt safer than

asking."

"I wanted her," he said, voice low. "I just didn't know how to. Every call felt urgent. I gave the best of me to the business and gave you what I thought you needed to survive."

"We survived."

"But you didn't thrive." Ethan ran a hand down his face. "I told myself I'd do more when things calmed down, but they never did."

"Not until you make them."

"Yeah," he looked around the room and then at her before reaching out to cradle her hand. "I didn't know how hard this was...especially alone."

The octopus bumped her wrist as she shifted. "We never figured out how to be parents together. No schedule. No plan. Holidays and awkward updates. I kept you at arm's length, and you didn't fight me on it."

"I didn't," he said. "I thought we were being polite. I was proud of how well we negotiated parenthood." He rubbed his thumb once at the base of her fingers. "It was lazy and cowardly."

"We can do better."

"We can't rewrite years, but I'd like to try to make up for some of it—like not being there to make lunches or handle 2 a.m. fevers."

"I'm not good at letting go," she said. "I don't want you to do it, but I want to figure out how to do it together."

"Share," he echoed. "And when I mess up—and I will—don't let me retreat to the office because it's easier."

Her mouth softened. "Then don't let me take over and

pretend I don't care when you get it wrong."

"Deal."

They sat in the hum and soft footfalls of the ward. The monitor kept its calm count. Down the hall, someone laughed, low and worn at the edges.

"Was Tiffany happy today?" Rowan asked, eyes on their hands.

A slow breath left him. "She called me Dad," he said.

Heat pricked under Rowan's eyes. She swallowed it back and turned her palm so their fingers threaded. "She doesn't give trust lightly."

"I know." He glanced down at the tiny octopus and huffed. "She gets that from both of us."

Something eased beneath her ribs. "Tell me more," she said, and it came out smaller than she intended.

He did. Not the highlight reel, just the ordinary moments she missed and wanted: the way Tiffany held on to his sleeve while they bought a ticket at the aquarium, how she fed fries to the seagulls, and the spelling words she struggled with the most.

"You sound...happy," Rowan said.

He blinked, surprised by his own answer. "I am."

The quiet that followed wasn't empty. It felt like something solid forming between them.

A nurse's cart rattled past, then the nurse reappeared with a glance at the clock and an apologetic lift of her brows.

"Time's up," she said, voice gentle. "Sorry to kick you out, but our patient needs her rest."

Ethan stood, reluctant and already stepping away. He reached for her, paused, then leaned in until their foreheads met—no heat, no hunger, only the clean press of skin to skin. His breath washed warm between them. The world narrowed to that point of contact.

"You're not alone," he said, low.

For a second, she let herself believe it without caveat or clause. She tilted into him, eyes closed, thumbs brushing. His hand lifted to cradle the back of her head, his thumb finding the ribbon of tension along her nape and easing it down.

The nurse cleared her throat in the doorway, trying—and failing—to hide her grin. "Don't make me call security."

Rowan's laugh tugged and held. "Busted."

Straightening, Ethan squeezed Rowan's fingers once before letting go. "I'll be back in the morning."

"Okay," Rowan said. "Tell Tiffany I'm proud of her."

"I will."

He stepped into the hall. The nurse guided him toward the elevators, leaving the curtain cracked. Rowan watched the triangle of light on the floor until it thinned and disappeared.

She looked at the octopus and at the hand-shaped warm patch on her blanket, cooling slowly.

"You're not alone," he said.

She lay back and let the thought hold. When sleep came, it felt less like surrender and more like choosing to rest while someone else kept watch.

Chapter Eight

Ethan

Tuesday morning arrived with all the grace of a freight train.

Ethan woke to the sound of his phone alarm screaming at six-thirty, and Fig perched on the armrest, her tail twitching in judgment.

A throw pillow crease smooshed his cheek, and the living room smelled like dryer sheets, crayons, and the faint metallic tang of old dust in the heater vents. A half-finished bracelet glimmered on the coffee table where sunlight nudged through the blinds. Small beads in teal and brass that Rowan had started to arrange into a little constellation and then wandered off mid-project.

"Good morning. I'm guessing you want food," he told Fig. She blinked and flicked her ear as if she was still measuring his worth before she jumped down to bat a hair tie across the kitchen floor like a tiny hockey puck.

He groaned, rolled off the couch, and found Tiffany already awake, sitting cross-legged on the living room rug with her backpack open and her library book balanced on her knees.

"Morning," he said.

She blinked at him, processing his presence like she did every morning—a small recalibration that he was still here, that this wasn't temporary. "Morning, Dad."

The word still caught him off guard, a little punch of warmth under his ribs that he hadn't fully earned but was determined to keep.

"I'll make some oatmeal," he said. "You want banana coins or—"

"We're out of bananas," she said, yawning. "Fig ate the last one."

He turned. "Fig ate a banana?"

"She licks them," Tiffany clarified. "Then nobody wants them."

He nodded and made a mental note to add bananas to the grocery list. "How do you feel about oatmeal with some brown sugar?"

She considered. "We can put peanut butter in it."

"Sounds...sticky."

He read the oats package while she rolled her eyes and reached for the bowls. When his fumbling dragged on, she took over, stabbing the microwave buttons with the confidence of a tiny engineer.

Ethan watched, doubtful that the breakfast would be edible. The cat circled warily before disappearing under the couch—clearly uncomfortable with the level of newness being forced upon her and the house.

Ethan couldn't help himself. "Hiding, huh? That Fig...ur

es."

Tiffany rolled her eyes but gave a small nod, granting him credit for the dad joke.

Removing the hot bowl when the microwave dinged, he stirred in a spoonful of peanut butter until the oatmeal loosened and turned glossy, then added a dash of cinnamon, pretending he knew what he was doing. The smell was warm and familiar, but the only core memory it stirred was of a generic hotel breakfast bar.

She scooped a bite and looked out the window over the kitchen sink. "I checked the weather app," she said. "It's supposed to rain. I need my pink jacket."

He blinked. "The one with the—"

"Heart on the pocket. In the closet."

She went back to her book, trusting him to handle it.

He found the jacket, smoothed the heart-patterned pocket once, and hung it near the heater to warm before school.

I've got you.

Instead of waiting in line, he found a spot three rows back and walked Tiffany to the entrance, her hand still tucked in his. Inside, the hallway buzzed with energy—children's laughter amplified by cinderblock walls and the squeak of rubber soles against freshly waxed linoleum.

At her classroom door, Tiffany waited for the line to clear.

Ethan inched forward, watched parents kiss foreheads and hand over almost forgotten lunch boxes, and felt the weight of being new at this settle across his shoulders.

When it was their turn to unload, Tiffany paused, one hand on the door handle.

"You'll be here at two forty-five?" she asked.

"Two-thirty," he said. "Early."

She studied his face, measuring the promise, then nodded. "Okay."

Tiffany started to pull away, then turned back and hugged him—quick and fierce, arms tight around his waist.

"Have a good day," he said.

"You too," she whispered, and disappeared into the classroom.

Ethan lingered at the edge of the hallway, watching until she disappeared, then started toward the exit.

He made it three steps before a cluster of moms intercepted him.

"Ethan, right?" The woman leading the pack had a bright smile and a travel mug that read 'Lowell Elementary PTA'. "Tiffany's Dad?"

"That's me," he said, slowing.

"Welcome to the chaos," she said warmly, though her eyes swept over him with an assessment usually reserved for contract reviews. "We haven't seen you around here before."

"I'm new to Seattle," he said, aiming for polite.

"Well, it's great that you're helping, now," another mom chimed in, her tone landing somewhere between supportive and pointed. "Rowan's been handling everything solo for so long. She's trying...and that's just...amazing."

Ethan nodded, sensing the compliment came with a side of

judgment he wasn't sure how to deflect.

The first mom tilted her head. "So, is Tiffany still planning to go to Lily's birthday party on Friday? We are confirming RSVPs."

"Yes," he said, grateful that he actually knew the answer. "In fact, we're making plans for her sister to be in town. I was hoping she could join, too."

The sharks at the aquarium looked less bloodthirsty. "Sister?" she asked.

"Yes, Rosie lives in Texas with her mother."

He wanted to tell them to stop whipping their heads around at each other, or they'd need a trip to the chiropractor. Instead, he smiled and pretended he didn't feel like chum in the water.

"Perfect," she said. "And you know it's at the trampoline park, right? The kids need socks, or you can buy them there. Drop-off is at four-thirty."

"Four-thirty," he repeated, mentally adding it to the list.

The second mom leaned in, conspiratorially. "And don't forget the craft club on Thursday. Tiffany signed up weeks ago. We're making friendship bracelets, so she'll need to bring a nut-free snack to share. Just something simple—fruit, crackers, nothing homemade unless you're feeling ambitious."

Ethan's mind scrambled. "Thursday. Craft club. Nut-free snack. Got it."

A third mom, quieter but no less observant, added, "It's at three, right after school. In the art room. They usually run for about an hour."

"Three o'clock," he said, nodding as if he'd known all along.

The first mom smiled. "You're doing great. It's a lot to keep track of."

Before he could respond, his phone buzzed in his pocket. Once. Twice. Three times in quick succession.

He pulled it out, glancing at the screen:

Sending an 11 a.m. EST MANDATORY meeting invite.

In the distributor meeting, we need your input NOW.

Call ASAP Urgent

The moms' eyes flickered to his vibrating phone.

"We should let you take that," the first one said, her smile tight at the corners as she stepped back. "Work emergencies, right? Always something."

The second mom's hand fluttered dismissively. "Don't worry about us. This parenting stuff takes practice."

The words landed like a quiet indictment. They didn't need to be loud to sting.

Heat crept up Ethan's neck. Clearly, his team had finally grown tired of covering for him. His thumb hovered over his phone when, across the hallway, Tiffany appeared in the classroom doorway, backpack still on. Her eyes skimmed the crowd until they found him, and her small shoulders loosened, just a little.

His phone buzzed again, the screen lighting up with another incoming call.

The moms shifted their weight, maintaining polite smiles that didn't quite reach their eyes.

Ethan looked from Tiffany's waiting face to the expectant mothers, then silenced the phone and pocketed it.

"Work can wait," he said, meeting the first mom's gaze.

Her eyebrows arched. "Well. That's...refreshing."

"Tiffany's lucky," the second mom added, sounding genuinely impressed.

"It's the other way around," Ethan said.

After quick goodbyes, he crossed to where Tiffany stood fidgeting with her backpack strap.

"You okay?" he asked, crouching to her level.

She nodded, fingers twisting the strap of her backpack. "I just...wanted to make sure."

"I'm here," he said. "Two-thirty pickup. Every day."

Her mouth curved into a small, tentative smile. "Okay."

"Okay," he echoed.

She turned and headed into the classroom, this time without looking back.

Ethan straightened and walked toward the exit, his phone already buzzing again in his pocket.

He let it ring.

The crisp morning breeze greeted him as he navigated the parking lot to his car. Once settled behind the wheel, he extracted his phone and assessed the damage.

Five missed calls. Three voicemails waiting. Multiple texts with escalating urgency. Harrison has sent all of them.

His jaw clenched as he studied the illuminated screen.

Then he typed a single message to the Ladder H sales lead.

Harrison. I'm in Seattle managing a family situation. Can take a virtual call in an hour. Let me know how you want to proceed.

He hit send before he could second-guess it.

The reply came within minutes.

We'll make it work remotely, but this isn't sustainable long-term. We need to discuss your availability going forward.

He exhaled, the tension in his shoulders easing a fraction.

Not sustainable. He was right.

But today wasn't about long-term. Today was about two-thirty, and craft club, and a birthday party on Friday that required a cool gift and not-ugly wrapping paper.

Today was about giving Rowan the help she deserved.

It was about bringing his girls together.

He pocketed the phone, started the car, and headed toward the hospital.

By the time he pulled into traffic, his phone was buzzing. There was another email from Harrison and a text from Bailey: *Rosie's flight is confirmed for tomorrow. She's coming in at 5:20 p.m I'll text you the gate info tonight.*

He waited for a stop sign before he typed back: *Thank you. I mean it.*

Her reply was instant: *Don't make me regret this.*

He wouldn't. He couldn't.

Chapter Nine

Ethan

Ethan's laptop bag had left a permanent indentation in the worn leather chair tucked against the exposed brick wall at Cool Beans. The coffee shop near the hospital was fast becoming his new office.

The barista—Mika, according to her name tag—nodded at him as he approached the counter for the third time that morning.

"Another Americano?" she asked, already reaching for a mug.

"Thanks." He slid three dollars into the tip jar.

He'd staked his claim in the back corner of the little shop two blocks from Seattle General. He could sprint to Rowan's room in under four minutes, and it was only seventeen minutes by car to Tiffany's school, accounting for afternoon traffic.

He nursed his third Americano—black, no room—and flipped open his laptop. His inbox refreshed with an ominous ping. *Urgent – Macallan Meeting* glared at him in bold, flagged with a red exclamation point that sent a knot twisting through his gut. Harrison needed to learn to chill.

Thursday's distribution planning meeting hung over him like an approaching thunderstorm. The hour he'd spent on the phone with the sales lead had only underscored how hard it was to be away from his job.

Dialing in remotely was an option, though not an ideal one. Brad, the new VP of sales, had practically jumped at the chance to step in when Ethan mentioned his situation, his eagerness setting off warning bells.

Clearly, Brad and Harrison were happy to shove him out of the discussion. But he'd worked at Ladder H for nearly two decades. Couldn't he take a leave? Couldn't he have a family? Sheesh.

What message would his absence send to the board, especially after the mess with Bailey and Rowan? Postponing until after Rowan recovered might cost them the Macallan account entirely. Either way, he'd be sacrificing something valuable.

He started to type—and stopped three times—before deleting the draft email. He'd have to think more about what he actually wanted to say to Brad.

His phone buzzed. He almost ignored it, assuming it was Harrison—but every text mattered now. It could be Rowan.

Kim: *Tiffany forgot her water bottle at my place. I'll bring it by after school. You holding up?*

He smiled despite himself: *Barely. Thanks for the backup.*

Kim: *Anytime. Rowan's lucky.*

He didn't know how to answer that, so he didn't. He closed the laptop, drained his coffee, and headed for the hospital.

Rowan was sitting up when he arrived. Loose tendrils of auburn hair curled around her shoulders, and there was a pink in her cheeks that had been missing at his last visit. She looked tired, but less like she was fighting for every breath.

"You're vertical," he said.

"Sort of," she said. "I did two laps this morning. Kelly threatened me with a third if I didn't eat all my lunch today."

He set a paper bag on the tray. "Herbal tea. Some fancy lavender honey kind from a cafe down the block."

"No hospital swill?" Her eyes lit up. "You're bribing me."

"Absolutely." He pulled the visitor chair close. "How are you feeling?"

"Like I got hit by a truck." She inhaled the steam rising from the cup he handed her, then took a careful sip. "This is heaven."

"So, it's good?"

"Perfect. Thank you..." She sipped, swallowed, and met his gaze. "How was your morning?"

"Flawless. If you ignore the chewy eggs and the fact that I almost forgot the purple packet at drop-off, again."

"But you didn't."

"But I didn't." He leaned back, shoulders easing. "Tiffany asked if I'd be there on time for pickup, again."

Rowan's expression softened. "She's learning to trust you."

"I'm learning to be trustworthy," he said quietly.

They sat in the hum of monitors and distant voices. Rowan finished the tea, placed the paper cup on the nearby tray, and reached for his hand without looking.

"You talked to Bailey? Rosie's coming?" she asked.

"Yeah. Tomorrow evening. I'm going to tell Tiffany tonight."

"Oh!"

"I'll pick Tiffany up from school and take her to get Rosie from the airport. They'll probably combust from excitement."

"Absolutely explode," Rowan said. She squeezed his fingers. "I'm glad you're doing this."

"They're sisters. It's good for them."

"I know...but we went so long the other way that I never expected us to be here. You know—"

"With them planning sleepovers and going to birthday parties together?"

"Yeah," she said. "Because I spent eight years not asking, and you spent eight years not offering. I know we're trying to do better."

He turned her hand over, thumb tracing the calluses at the base of her fingers—the small, earned marks of her work. "Then let's keep trying."

Kelly appeared with a tray of pills and a knowing smile. "Aw, aren't you two a sight," she said cheerfully. "Time for meds and another lap." She pointed at Ethan, "You can walk with her if you promise to keep it slow."

"Yes, ma'am," he said.

Rowan laughed, winced, and let him help her stand.

They walked slowly down the hallway, her hand light on his arm, steps careful but steady. At the end of the corridor, she paused by the window overlooking the parking lot.

"Ethan?"

"Yeah?"

"When I get out of here, I want to make dinner. A family dinner for all of us."

He looked at her, backlit by winter sun, hospital gown tied crooked, and felt something shift in his chest that had nothing to do with panic or obligation.

"Deal," he said.

She smiled, and they turned back toward her room, one slow step at a time.

That evening, after Tiffany finished her homework, Ethan checked the kitchen clock: 5:15 p.m. Right on schedule. He'd managed school pickup without a hitch and dinner without a fire alarm.

"Tiffany," he said, leaning his hip against the counter. "I talked to Rosie's mom today."

She looked up from her coloring book, marker paused mid-air. "Did something happen?"

"No," he said quickly. Then he smiled. "Nothing bad. I was wondering how you'd feel about Rosie coming to visit. She's on spring break."

Her eyes widened. "Here?"

"Here," he confirmed. "For an entire week, if that still sounds good to you."

She didn't answer—she launched. Her chair scraped back, and she crossed the kitchen in a blur, wrapping her arms around his waist.

"Yes. Yes. Yes." She tipped her head back to look at him. "When?"

"Tomorrow."

That did it. She bolted down the hall.

She dragged the folding cot out of the hall closet. "Rosie likes pink," she announced, retrieving a ruffled comforter that probably hadn't seen daylight in years. She arranged her one-eyed unicorn—long bequeathed the name Shimmer Star, he'd learned—against the pillow with careful grace. The cotton-candy bedding looked almost defiant beneath Tiffany's glow-in-the-dark solar system and the framed Mars rover poster that hung above her bed.

"I can't wait until we have a slumber party!"

"You're going to need some sleep before the party starts," Ethan said, smiling as he crossed the room. "Otherwise, you won't make it through the pillow fights."

She grinned, unrepentant. "I won't be tired."

"That's what everyone says," he said, steering her gently toward her dresser. "Teeth. Pajamas. Then you can tell me everything you're planning for The Best Sleepover Ever."

She bounced once on her toes, then darted for the bathroom, already narrating ideas over her shoulder.

Ethan lingered a moment, taking in the pink quilt on the cot, the careful way she'd placed the unicorn, the space she'd made without being asked. On Rosie's previous visits, Bailey had always kept the girls' worlds separate—hotel rooms, day trips, and carefully scheduled playdates.

Tomorrow would mark uncharted territory: seven days,

two girls, one townhouse.

Half-sisters becoming just sisters, maybe.

The thought terrified and thrilled him equally.

Chapter Ten

Rowan

Rowan woke to low voices outside her door and the soft shuffle of paper.

"…cultures aren't back yet," one said. "Her white count dipped, then ticked up this morning."

"Keep the IV antibiotics. Watch the drain output. I don't love the low-grade fever. She stays until we're past it."

She stared at the ceiling tile with the faint stain shaped like a teapot, jaw tight. *Staying.* Not heading home tonight. *Here longer.*

When Dr. Cole stepped in—composed, kind—Rowan had already tucked her hands under the blanket to hide how tightly they clenched.

"Hi, Ms. Fontaine." He checked the monitor, then met her gaze. "You're improving, but not as quickly as we hoped. Today's labs show some inflammation hanging on. We're going to keep you for a few more days. It's not a setback. It's a precaution."

"Another few days," she said, tongue sticking to the words.

"I know it isn't what you want to hear," he said. "We're keeping you safe." He ran through the plan in simple steps: antibiotics, hall walks, expanding her diet past liquids if her stomach agreed, and then more labs again in the morning. "Any questions?"

"Only a thousand that won't change anything," she said, shooting for wry and landing near raw.

"You'll be on the other side of this soon." He lowered a hand on the rail, brief and steady, then he slipped back into the hallway hum.

A light knock. Ethan's head appeared around the curtain, hair damp from the rain outside, jacket dark at the shoulders. In his hand: a small bundle of ranunculus in cheerful coral and cream, wrapped in brown paper and twine.

"I checked," he said before she could protest. "No lilies. Nurse Kelly gave me a lecture and then a vase."

He set them on the windowsill where the light could find them, then came to the bed.

"You look like you got news," he said softly.

"I'm apparently a fan favorite," she said, trying for light and not quite getting there. "They want to keep me a few more days. Fever bumped. Inflammation's being stubborn."

"Okay." He pulled the visitor's chair closer and leaned in, elbows on his knees. "Then we plan around that."

"I hate that sentence," she said. "I hate all of this."

"I know." He let the quiet hold for a beat. "I can see if they'll let me sleep here tonight."

"On that torture device they call a chair? No."

"It can't be worse than your couch."

That put a short-lived smile on her face, then she shook her head once. "You need to sleep, and Tiffany needs you more than I do."

His mouth tipped, then the concern in his eyes, quiet and real, pushed past her frustration.

"You didn't sleep last night," she said.

"I've slept," he lied, and they both knew it.

"I'd rather be alone here than have Tiff without a parent."

He breathed out, releasing the argument he'd been prepared to deliver because he knew she was right. "Then I'll go back to her after dinner. Kim can help. I'll come early tomorrow, and we'll call you before school."

"Thank you," she said, and meant it. "She's scared. She'll act like she isn't, but she is. Don't let her be too brave."

"She's just like her mom." He rubbed a thumb along his knuckles—a restless tell. "Bailey and I are on track with Rosie. Tiffany is already moving around furniture in her room."

Warmth moved through Rowan so fast it felt like relief and grief in one pass. "Yes," she said, the word leaving her in a rush. "It will be so much better."

"We can manage the week," he said. "Drop-offs. Homework. The birthday party. The invitation's on the fridge."

"You remembered the craft day?"

"Thursday at three."

"You'll need snacks," she said. "And patience."

"I'm short on none of the above." He reached for a paper bag on the tray and pulled out a warm tea for her.

She sipped, closed her eyes, and let the heat settle. "This is heaven."

"So, it's good?"

"Perfect." She opened her eyes and found him watching her with something she couldn't quite name—relief, and something softer. "Thank you."

"How are you feeling?"

"Like I got hit by a truck," she said, taking another sip. "But a smaller truck than yesterday."

They sat in the hum of monitors and the inaudible murmurs from the hall. She finished half the tea, set it aside, and her hand found his without thinking. His fingers curled around hers, warm and solid.

"How was your morning?" she asked.

"Flawless," he said. "If you ignore the cat licked banana and the fact that Tiffany had to let me know it was going to rain today."

"She's learning to trust you."

"I'm learning to be trustworthy," he said, voice low.

She studied their joined hands—his broad and capable, hers smaller, marked with tiny nicks from years of wire and metal. She squeezed his fingers. "Thank you for doing this."

"You don't have to keep thanking me."

"I do," she said, before a sharp stab of pain left her breath short. He helped her settle against the pillows, his hand lingering at her elbow a beat longer than necessary.

"You okay?"

"Getting there." She glanced at the tray table, where a covered meal sat beside her pills. "They brought me actual food. Not broth."

"Progress," he said, and lifted the lid. Steam rose from roasted chicken, mashed potatoes, and green beans so limp that they looked like they'd been cooked sometime last week.

"Share it with me?"

"A few bites." He split the plate and rotated the side with more chicken toward her. "I'm getting tired of my own cooking."

They ate in companionable silence, forks scraping the institutional plate and brushing against one another as they ate. Even when they'd been officially together, they'd never shared this kind of ordinary. Not even when she was pregnant. Back then, her changing body had seemed to scare him away more than bring him closer. This settled over her like a weight—domestic, familiar, married-adjacent—and it didn't terrify her.

"Tiffany has been anxious," he said. "She overplans and worries about forgetting things."

"She's always worried a bit when her routine changes."

"Yeah." He hesitated. "She told me she's excited to see Rosie. She called her 'my sister.'"

Air left Rowan's lungs. She looked down, blinking against the sting. Tiffany was cautious with affection, guarded with hope. Hearing that she'd claimed Rosie—not hesitantly, but as fact—meant something had shifted.

Since the day she'd conceived Tiffany, she'd known about Rosie. But Rosie and Bailey had only learned about Tiffany recently, and she had only recently told her daughter about Rosie.

"That's...good," she said.

"It is," he said.

"For the birthday party," she added, voice steadier. "Can you manage getting a gift?"

"I'll take both girls to the toy store and let them pick."

She bit back a smile, already picturing the chaos. "That should be...enlightening."

"You're laughing at me in your head," he said.

"Absolutely."

They finished eating. He stacked the dishes and cleaned up. She shifted and finally admitted how much space he took up in this small, sterile room—and how much she wanted him to stay.

"Ethan?"

"Yeah?"

"When I was waiting for surgery, I was sure she was going to end up scared and alone and angry at me."

He went still. Then, without thinking, he tucked a strand of hair behind her ear. His fingers lingered against her cheekbone, warm and deliberate.

"She wasn't alone," he said.

Everything tightened—the air, the space between them, the careful distance they'd kept. Rowan turned into his touch instead of away, breath catching as their faces drew close.

Not drunk close. Not reckless close. *Intentional.*

For a heartbeat, it felt inevitable.

The door swung open with a cheerful squeak. Kelly bustled in to check the IV bag, grin widening when she saw them.

"Boyfriend duty again?" she teased.

Ethan pulled back, throat working. Rowan didn't correct her. Kelly finished her checks and left with a wink that said she knew exactly what she'd interrupted.

The air had changed—softer and sharper at once. Rowan studied Ethan—exhaustion carved at the corners of his eyes, his shoulders carrying a weight that hadn't been there a week ago.

"Are you holding up?" she asked.

He smiled; it didn't reach his eyes. "Well enough."

She didn't believe him, but she didn't push either.

His phone alarm went off. "It's two. I can't be late."

When he stood, he squeezed her hand—not just casually or politely. But a promise to come back.

"Goodbye, Rowan."

"Goodbye."

He stepped through the curtain. It sighed shut.

Rowan settled deeper into the pillow. The room hummed—IV pump, monitor, the soft squeak of rubber soles in the hall. Quiet took the edges off.

She drifted in and out for a while until a notification vibrated her phone and lit up the screen.

Tiffany: *Rosie's bed is ready. Dad said I could pick the blanket. Do you think she'll like it?*

Rowan stared at the photo until her vision blurred.

Rowan: *Baby, she's going to love it. You're a good sister.*

Tiffany: *I want her to feel at home. Dad said that's important.*

Dad. The word had slid into Tiffany's vocabulary like it had always been waiting.

Rowan: *He's right. You both are doing something special.*

Tiffany: *Do you think we'll be okay? All of us together?*

Rowan closed her eyes and breathed through the ache in her ribs.

Rowan: *I think you're already okay. You're already a family.*

The pause stretched.

Then, Tiffany sent: *I miss you, Mom.*

Rowan: *I miss you too, sweetheart. And I'm proud of you. You're being brave and kind, and you're taking care of people you love. That's everything.*

Tiffany: *Ethan says we're doing good.*

Rowan: *You are. All of you.*

Tiffany: *Goodnight, Mom. Love you to the moon and back.*

Rowan: *To the moon and back, baby. Always.*

She set the phone aside and pressed her palms to her face. The photo stayed open—pink comforter, stuffed unicorn, a cot set up for a sister landing tomorrow.

Half-sisters turning into just sisters.

It should have scared her. Instead, it settled warm and solid in her chest. She'd spent eight years holding the world together alone, convinced that asking for help was failure.

It was something she'd never let herself imagine: *a family that didn't hinge on her holding every piece by herself.*

She reached for her phone again.

Rowan: *It was nice to see you today.*

Ethan: *You, too...*

Rowan: *I'm glad we're trying.*

Ethan: *Me, too.*

She smiled despite the ache in her side, tucked the blanket around her knees, and let herself rest—not because she was giving up, but because she was learning to trust that when she woke, the people she loved would still be there.

Chapter Eleven

Ethan

Overhead speakers crackled with gate changes and final boarding calls while roller bags rumbled across the terminal's gleaming tiles. The air hung heavy with that unmistakable airport cocktail—stale breath from a thousand travelers, duty-free perfume wafting from shopping bags, and the greasy ghost of lingering fast-food smells.

Ethan stood at the arrivals gate with Tiffany's hand tucked into his, watching the stream of passengers flood through the sliding doors. Tiffany had gone quiet the moment they'd entered the terminal—not scared quiet, but the tense, waiting quiet of a kid who'd built something up so big in her mind that reality couldn't possibly match.

"What if she doesn't remember me?" Tiffany whispered.

Ethan squeezed her hand. "She remembers you. And if she forgot anything, you'll remind her in about thirty seconds."

Tiffany's mouth twitched, almost a smile.

The crowd thickened—businessmen in rumpled suits,

families dragging oversized luggage, a woman in yoga pants jug-
gling a coffee and a screaming toddler. Then, cutting through
the chaos, a uniformed attendant appeared, gripping eye hand
of a small blonde missile.

"Mr. Moore?"

Rosie was already pulling the attendant towards him when
he nodded and waved to get her attention.

The woman consulted her clipboard. "ID, please."

Ethan fumbled for his wallet while Rosie bounced on her
toes, backpack half-unzipped, one strap sliding off her shoulder. Her hair had escaped whatever Bailey had attempted that
morning and stood in wild curls around her face.

"DAD!" she shrieked the moment the attendant nodded
and released her hand.

She didn't hesitate. She didn't pause. She full-on launched
herself upward, her small body practically vibrating with excitement as she leaped from the attendant's side.

Ethan braced himself half a second before she collided with
his chest, arms and legs wrapping around him like a koala.
He caught her with a laugh that surprised him—helpless and
full-bodied and utterly unguarded.

"Hi, kiddo."

"I missed you soooo much," Rosie said into his shoulder,
squeezing hard enough to make his ribs complain. "The plane
had tiny pretzels, but they were stale, ew, and the lady next to
me snored, and I watched two movies, and one was about a dog
who could *talk*."

Ethan set her down gently and crouched so he was eye level
with both girls. Tiffany stood half a step back, watching Rosie

with a mix of awe and wariness—like she wasn't sure if her sister was a force of nature or a natural disaster.

"Rosie," Ethan said, keeping his voice steady. "You remember Tiffany."

Rosie turned, and for one precarious second, Ethan held his breath.

Then Rosie grinned, wide and gap-toothed. "Hi! I brought you gummy bears, but I ate the red ones on the plane because they're the best." She dug into her jacket pocket and produced a crumpled bag. "Also, do you like slime?"

Tiffany blinked. Then, in a voice barely above a whisper: "I love slime. My mom hates it. She says it's almost as bad as glitter, but not quite."

Rosie gasped as if Tiffany had just revealed the secret to world peace. "That's exactly what my mom says!"

Just like that, the temperature shifted. Tiffany's shoulders dropped. Rosie bounced on her toes. And Ethan, watching them find each other in the middle of SeaTac Airport, felt something loosen in his chest. He'd been bracing and didn't know how hard until he didn't have to anymore.

"Alright," he said, standing and reaching for Rosie's backpack. "Let's get out of here before I misplace one of you."

The car ride started crazy and stayed that way.

Rosie talked nonstop about the flight, about the dog movie, about how Bailey had packed her three kinds of snacks because it was the first time she was flying really far all alone. Tiffany listened, wide-eyed, occasionally interjecting with questions that Rosie answered with an authority only a nine-year-old could muster.

"So, your mom runs a whole company?" Tiffany asked.

"Yep. I mean, Dad helps, but she's the boss of everyone."

Ethan glanced in the rearview mirror and caught Tiffany's small smile. She was relaxing, he realized. Not all the way—Tiffany didn't do anything halfway—but enough.

"So," Ethan said, "to celebrate the first real sister hangout, we need to knock out some practical dad tasks."

Both girls looked at him as if he'd just announced naptime.

"We're going to the toy store," he continued. "For Lily's birthday party. You two get to pick the present."

Rosie's eyes getting huge. "We get to pick?"

"Within reason," Ethan said quickly, already regretting his phrasing.

"What's reason?" Rosie asked.

"Something that won't make Lily's parents hate me." He thought for a moment, "Or your mom."

Tiffany leaned forward. "Lily really wants the glitter unicorn karaoke machine."

Ethan's hands tightened on the steering wheel. "The what?"

"I've heard of them, but never seen one. It's pink, and it has a microphone and a special button so that, when you finish a song, glitter shoots out the horn," Rosie said, her voice climbing with excitement. "That sounds amazing!"

"That sounds like a noise complaint waiting to happen," Ethan muttered.

Tiffany gave him a look—flat and unimpressed in a way that

reminded him uncomfortably of Rowan. "Dad. It's a birthday."

Rosie nodded. "She's right."

Ethan sighed and took the exit toward the shopping center.

The toy store was an explosion of sounds and primary colors.

Ethan followed the girls down aisles packed with dolls, board games, and things that beeped for no discernible reason. Rosie grabbed a shopping basket, and Tiffany trailed behind, pointing out options with the seriousness of a procurement specialist.

"What about this?" Rosie held up a build-your-own robot kit.

"Lily doesn't like robots," Tiffany said. "She likes art."

"Boring." Rosie drawled.

"It's not boring, it's sophisticated."

Ethan stepped between them before the debate could escalate. "How about we find something you both agree on?"

They exchanged a look—some wordless sister negotiation he wasn't privy to—and then took off toward the craft aisle.

Five minutes later, they returned holding a sparkly zip case filled with markers, colored pencils, and stickers that proclaimed things like "YOU'RE A STAR" and "SLAY QUEEN."

"This," Tiffany announced, "is perfect."

"It's fancy *and* fun," Rosie added. "We negotiated."

Ethan looked at the price tag and tried not to wince. "Negotiated. Right."

In the parking lot, Ethan loaded the bag into the trunk and

turned to find both girls watching him expectantly.

"Now what?" he asked.

"Dinner," Tiffany said. "But not anything Dad tries to cook."

Rosie, curious, asked, "Is he bad at cooking?"

"He burnt broccoli."

"Broccoli?" Rosie looked genuinely horrified. "Good thing New York has a lot of restaurants."

Ethan held up his hands in mock surrender. "Okay. I get it. My cooking skills could use some work. Where do you two want to eat?"

They looked at each other, grinned, and said in perfect unison: "The Old Spaghetti Factory."

The restaurant buzzed with cozy chaos—warm air, high ceilings, and the constant clatter of silverware echoing through the room. Every table was full, kids chattering and laughing without a care, and no one blinked when a breadstick skittered across the floor. It was a place where messes were expected, and memories were made.

They'd squeezed into a booth, Ethan on one side, both girls on the other. A server appeared with crayons and a kid's menu shaped like a conductor's hat, and covered in games and a choo-choo train cartoon. Rosie immediately started drawing what she claimed was "a picture of Dad," but it looked more like a stick figure with angry eyebrows.

"Flattering," Ethan said.

"You have resting grump face," Rosie informed him.

Tiffany giggled into her hand.

When the food arrived—meaty mac and cheese for the girls, brown butter mizithra for Ethan—Rosie launched into a story about a friend in New York who'd tried to pierce her own ears with a sewing needle and an ice cube.

Ethan choked on his water. "She WHAT?"

"It didn't work," Rosie said cheerfully. "Her mom found out, and she got grounded for, like, a year."

"Good," Ethan said, still coughing.

Tiffany leaned in, eyes wide. "Did it hurt?"

"Probably," Rosie said. "But she said it was worth it."

The conversation spiraled from there. They covered every topic from school stories to favorite animals—Rosie's was her goat, and Tiffany loved orcas—and they ended with a heated debate about whether glitter was an acceptable craft supply or a crime against humanity.

"It gets everywhere," Tiffany said.

"That's the point," Rosie countered. "It's like...a sparkle surprise for weeks."

Ethan watched them, these two girls who'd barely known each other a year ago, now talking over each other and stealing bites of garlic bread from the same plate. Their legs knocked under the table. Their laughter overlapped.

He pulled out his phone and snapped a quick photo—both girls leaning over one bowl, foreheads nearly touching, smiling so wide their eyes disappeared.

He sent it to Rowan with a simple caption: *Our first meal together.*

Her reply came almost instantly: *Oh.*

Then, after a pause, *tell them I love them. Tell Rosie thank you for coming. Tell Tiffany I'm so happy she has her sister there with her.*

Ethan read the messages aloud. Tiffany's eyes became bright and soft at the same time. Rosie, without missing a beat, said, "We got you, Mom."

With a small statement, Rowan wasn't just Tiffany's mom anymore. She was both of theirs.

The drive home was quieter.

Rosie fought sleep in the backseat, her chin bobbing as she tried to keep up a running commentary about Friday's birthday party. "And then we have to make sure the wrapping paper isn't ugly, I want a sister day, and Thursday is craft day after school—"

"A sister day!" Rosie echoed from the other side of the backseat, her voice confident.

Tiffany nodded, eyes already drifting closed. Then, without warning, her head tipped sideways and came to rest on Rosie's shoulder.

Rosie froze for half a second, like she wasn't sure what to do. Then, gently, she leaned her own head against Tiffany's, creating a small bridge between them.

In the rearview mirror, Ethan watched them—two girls, half-asleep, holding each other up without even thinking about it.

Something tightened in his chest, a bittersweet ache for all the moments like this he'd missed, and all the ones that might still come.

Back at the townhouse, Ethan's dream of a quiet evening evaporated.

"Is this cot bouncy or stabby?" Rosie demanded, poking the thin cot mattress with suspicion as she fired questions about bathroom schedules and where to store her backpack. Tiffany appointed herself official in-house ambassador, whispering "Fig hides behind the couch when she's scared" and "This is the perfect cartoon-watching spot" as they moved from room to room.

The toothbrushing marathon involved foamy spit, a vanished cap, and Ethan's stern "Rinse, don't swallow." He surprised himself by getting through four chapters of the bear book—complete with voices that made Rosie's eyes roll even as she grinned—before tucking both girls in with unexpected smoothness.

"Goodnight, Dad," Tiffany whispered from her bed.

"Goodnight, Dad," came Rosie's echo, her voice already clouded with sleep.

From the doorway, Ethan watched their breathing settle into a rhythm. Shimmer Star nestled between their beds like a plush guardian. His shoulders had just relaxed when a small voice broke the dim silence.

"Dad? Can I have some water?"

He let out a laughing sigh. "Okay, one glass of water on the way."

When he finally dropped onto the couch and checked his phone, the day's Ladder H messages glowed accusingly, still marked urgent, still waiting for replies.

He scrolled past them and opened a new text to Rowan: *They're asleep. They're okay. You can rest.*

Her reply came quickly: *Thank you.* Then, after a pause: *How does it feel?*

He stared at those words until his vision blurred, then he typed two words: *Scary. Perfect.*

Then he set the phone aside, stretched out on the couch, and let exhaustion pull him under.

Chapter Twelve

Ethan

Ethan woke on the couch to find both girls already awake, huddled in Tiffany's doorway as if they were planning a heist. Rosie's hair stuck up at wild angles. Tiffany still wore her star-patterned pajamas, but her backpack sat ready by the door.

"Morning," he said, voice rough from sleep.

Two heads swiveled toward him in perfect synchronization.

"We have a system," Rosie announced.

"A system," Ethan repeated, pushing himself upright.

"For school mornings," Tiffany clarified. "Rosie's got a plan."

"Okay..." Ethan braced himself to manage the master plan of a nine-year-old. "Let me know how I can help."

He'd expected chaos—fighting over the bathroom, tears over tangled hair, the sibling warfare that required diplomatic intervention. Instead, what he got was Rosie marching Tiffany to the bathroom mirror with the confidence of a drill sergeant.

"One long braid," Rosie declared, already sectioning

Tiffany's hair with her fingers. "It's a power move. Trust me."

Tiffany sat perfectly still on the closed toilet lid, hands folded in her lap. "Mom usually does two."

"Two is baby braids," Rosie said with the authority of someone barely a year older. "One is business."

Ethan leaned against the doorframe and watched Rosie's small fingers work through the strands. Her efforts were clumsy but determined, as the braid angled slightly to the left but held together. When she finished, she stepped back and surveyed her work with the critical eye of a seasoned professional.

"There. You look ready to conquer the world."

Tiffany gently touched the braid, then smiled. "Thanks, Rosie."

"Dad, don't forget Tiffany's water bottle," Rosie called from the table.

He grabbed it from the dish rack. "Got it."

"And she needs her library book for in-class reading today."

"On it." He found the book on the coffee table, checked the due date stamped inside, and slid it into Tiffany's backpack.

Rosie looked up from her eggs, eyebrows raised. "You're doing pretty good."

"High praise from the expert," he said.

"It's easy." Rosie shrugged. "WWMD?"

Ethan just stared at her.

"What would Mom do?"

When it was time to leave, Tiffany hesitated at the door, that familiar flicker of anxiety crossing her face. But then Rosie appeared at her elbow, backpack slung over one shoulder, grinning like she owned the world.

"Ready?" Rosie asked.

Tiffany nodded, and they walked to the car together.

At drop-off, Tiffany didn't cling to his sleeve or check three times that he'd be there at pickup.

Instead, she walked through the doors with her sister at her side.

Rosie waved at random kids as if she'd been attending Lowell Elementary her entire life. She radiated the bossy nine-year-old confidence that made other children either scatter or fall in line.

At the classroom door, Tiffany glanced back once. Ethan lifted his hand in a small wave.

She smiled and disappeared inside.

Rosie lingered in the hallway, watching the younger kids file past with the quiet assessment of someone taking mental notes. "She's gonna be fine," she said.

"I know," Ethan said. "Thank you for your help."

"Sure. I am a big sister, now." Rosie put on a serious face and glanced toward Tiffany's classroom.

Ethan dropped to a knee and held out his hand to pull her a little closer. "Being a big sister is a pretty big responsibility," he said, pausing for a moment while she nodded. "But, you don't have to do it all on your own. Rowan and I can take some of the hits."

"I know, Dad, but you're learning, too."

"I am," he said, pulling her into a hug. "Good thing I'm a

fast learner!"

Rosie laughed when he gave her a gentle squeeze. "Now." She tugged on his jacket. "Can we get bubble tea? Tiffany said it's a West Coast thing and I need to try it."

He checked his watch. They had time before he needed to tackle the day's errands. "Bubble tea it is."

The bubble tea shop was tucked between a nail salon and a vintage record store, its windows plastered with bright posters advertising flavors Ethan couldn't pronounce. Inside, the air smelled of sugar and fruit, and a chalkboard menu stretched across the back wall in looping pastel script.

Rosie pressed her nose to the glass display case, eyes wide. "There are so many choices."

"Pick one," Ethan said. "Just not the one with the most sugar. Your mom will kill me."

She squinted at the menu, lips moving as she read. "Mango with lychee jelly."

"Done."

They ordered—mango for Rosie and black tea (without bubbles) for Ethan—and settled at a small table by the window. Rosie stabbed her straw through the plastic lid with more force than necessary and took a long, dramatic sip.

Her eyes went wide. "It's... um... *chunky*."

"That's the point," Ethan said.

"They're squishy." She chewed thoughtfully. "I kind of like them."

He watched her take another sip, cheeks hollowing as she sucked up a cluster of lychee lumps. This was new territory—just him and Rosie, no Bailey mediating, no carefully scheduled cross-country handoffs. Just a Thursday morning in a bubble tea shop, and his daughter grinning at him over a cup of mango-flavored liquid sunshine.

"Down to business," he said, pulling a folded list from his pocket. "We have a mission today."

Rosie perked up. "A mission?"

"We're setting ourselves up for success this week," Ethan said, his tone so serious it made her smile.

She leaned forward, elbows on the table. "What are we doing?"

"Heading to the grocery store. We need to figure out how to make something other than pasta for dinner.

Rosie nodded solemnly. "Good plan."

Lured by convenience, Ethan reached for a box of mac and cheese, only to have Rosie pluck it from his hand.

"No neon-orange foods," she said, replacing it with a more naturally colored whole-grain version. "Tiffany said healthy foods."

"Your mother brainwashed you," Ethan muttered.

"Yeah, well, gouda is gooda," Rosie said without missing a beat.

"Did you just—" He stared at her.

"Mom says it all the time." She grinned. "It's a cheese joke."

They filled the cart with vegetables, rice, and a rotisserie chicken because Ethan knew his limits.

Rosie added a bag of apples and a bunch of bananas—"To replace the ones Fig licked"—and they moved toward the checkout.

At the register, Ethan's phone buzzed. He pulled it out and saw Rowan's name on the screen.

"Hold on," he said to Rosie, then answered. "Hey."

"Hey." Rowan's voice was soft, a little breathless. "How's the morning going?"

"Good. Great, actually." He glanced at Rosie, who was watching him with interest. "Rosie's here. Want to say hi?"

He switched to speakerphone and held the microphone between them.

"Hey, kid. Thanks for helping your dad," Rowan said.

"Hi, Rowan!" Rosie's face lit up. "Sure! Tiffany got to school great. She only cried for a minute because she missed you, but then I said, 'Sisters got this,' and Dad remembered lunch snacks without me even telling him."

Rowan's laugh came through the speaker, warm and surprised. "Thank you, hun, and thank you for taking care of Tiffany."

"Obviously," Rosie said. "I'm the big sister."

Ethan took the phone back. "We're at the grocery store. Should be back at the townhouse in an hour or so."

"Okay." There was a pause, and he could hear the smile in her voice. "You're surprising me, Ethan."

"Trying to," he said.

"I can tell."

After they hung up, Rosie looked up at him. "She sounds happy."

"Yeah," Ethan said. "She does."

Chapter Thirteen

Ethan

Any confidence Ethan had gone to bed with had thinned by morning. The night before had been warm and loud and full—a shared meal, Rosie's running commentary, Tiffany's laugh drifting down the hall. By daylight, all of it felt out of reach.

The calls he'd been avoiding couldn't be put off any longer. Whatever pocket of grace he'd carved out with Brad and Harrison had closed overnight.

He'd tried to reschedule. He'd even let the phone ring once too long, watching the screen until it went dark. But Harrison called again, and this time Ethan answered.

"Are you sure this will work?" Harrison said, tie crooked, voice tinny through the speaker. "This needs to go well."

"I'll dial in and prep the deck," Ethan said. "You'll have what you need."

Ethan chose Cool Beans for the call because the brick wall behind the two-top read better on camera than Rowan's thrifted couch and a glitter-covered coffee table. He wiped at a faint ring on the wood, then angled his laptop to kill the glare from the cafe's large picture window.

Across from him, Rosie sipped from a mango bubble tea—her new favorite beverage. She hadn't needed a bribe to wait patiently, but he'd bought her one, anyway.

She knew the drill. Nearly two years of watching Bailey run a company had trained her for this. She spread her markers out in a row in front of her and wrote an agenda at the top of her notepad—Hospital. Gift. Party socks.

Once she was in full admin mode, she glanced around the room like a tiny librarian, shushing a loud table near the window with a single, withering look.

The meeting opened hot. Numbers. Timelines. Positions.

"Can you give us a status summary, Ethan?" a board member asked.

"I'm in Seattle for an emergency family medical situation," Ethan said, steady. "So I'm not in the Manhattan conference room, but I'm ready to walk the distributor deck."

He shared his screen. Clean slides. Tight copy. No fluff.

"Let's keep the first three pallets on a thirty-day reorder cadence. We'll cover the initial display build and the tiered back-end swap-in: three points at 90 days, five at 120 if they hit pull-through. In return, we want feature ads in week one and adult-bev endcaps in week three. We rotate SKUs so nothing naps on the shelf."

"Slotting?" someone asked.

"Covered on the first drop only," he said. "We're not paying a cover charge to stand in the room all season."

Harrison cleared his throat. "Ethan, are you sure you can't be here in person to run this?"

"I can run it from here without dropping the ball," he said. "You've got me for the strategy and the math. That's the job."

Under the screen, Rosie slid him a small thumbs-up, then drew a fat checkmark next to Hospital and shot him the same time-is-ticking look his assistant used to give him.

A buyer from the distributor cut in. "Your margin's tight at $59. Freight's not doing you favors."

"We'll make it back on movement," Ethan said. "And we trim the sampler to four bottles to cut glass. Freight comes down, trial stays up. If we don't see lift by week two, we switch and push tastings with the second pallet."

He let the silence sit. On the laptop's speakers, someone exhaled.

"That could work," a voice said. "Send the revised three-month, broken out by chain."

"On your desk by morning," Ethan said.

Harrison's box reappeared. "We need you in the room next week."

Ethan kept his tone even. "I can prep the deck and lead the call. If you need a body at the head of the table, you've got this, Harry."

Across the table, a man at the window got loud again. Rosie turned, lifted a finger to her lips, and gave him a look so fierce he blinked, apologized to no one in particular, and lowered his voice. Rosie gave Ethan a prim nod.

He took the opening. "One more thing—if we want locations to say yes on placements, we give them an easy win. Offer a single-store trial with a guaranteed pickup clause. If they don't sell through, we swap for our top mover. It won't get exercised, and they'll feel covered."

The buyer spoke first this time. "We'll look into the numbers you mentioned." A beat. "We're looking forward to meeting in person."

The call ended with a chorus of goodbyes and the polite click that always sounded like someone closing a door from far away.

Ethan closed his laptop and rolled his shoulders as the espresso machine hummed back into focus. *Time check. Discharge papers. Curb lane. Two kids. Socks. Gift.*

Rosie pushed her agenda across the table. She'd circled the hospital twice. "You did good," she said, matter-of-factly. Then, slower, "They want you to go to New York."

"I heard." He capped his pen and tucked it into his notebook.

"We could call Mom—"

"Don't you dare." He stood, slid the laptop into his bag, and held out his hand. "Let's go get lunch, and then it will be time to pick up Tiffany."

"And get ready for the library craft."

He'd been trying to forget about library craft time all day. He'd take a dozen board meetings, but running a craft circle felt daunting.

"I'm there for moral support, buying supplies, and clean up. You and Tiffany are taking the lead on this one."

"Fine," Rosie said, rolling her eyes. "It's just a beading craft."

She took his hand and looked up at him before they started heading towards the door. He couldn't tell if she was offering him comfort or just leading him to his doom.

By day two of Rosie running school pickup, it ran like a well-oiled machine.

Ethan pulled into the parking lot at two-thirty sharp, Rosie riding shotgun and bouncing in her seat. They'd spent the afternoon at home folding laundry and trying not to wake Fig, who'd claimed the sunny spot on the couch like a furry tyrant.

"There!" Rosie pointed through the windshield as the first wave of kids poured through the double doors.

Tiffany appeared in the middle of the pack, backpack bouncing against her shoulders, ponytail swinging. When she spotted them, her entire face opened—eyes bright, mouth splitting into a grin that made something warm settle in Ethan's chest.

She didn't walk. She ran.

Straight across the blacktop, past the parent volunteers with their clipboards, past the crossing guard waving cars through. She barreled toward them.

Rosie was out of the car the second Ethan shifted into park.

The collision happened on the sidewalk—Tiffany launching herself at Rosie with enough force to make them both stumble. Their arms tangled, laughter spilling out in breathless hiccups, backpacks swinging wildly.

"You're here! Did you guys have fun today? I missed you!"

Tiffany said, squeezing Rosie hard enough to wrinkle her jacket. "I wish I could stay home with you."

"Obviously," Rosie said, squeezing back just as fiercely.

Ethan stood by the open car door, watching them hold each other like they'd been separated for years instead of hours. Other parents glanced over—some smiled, a few looked curious—but he didn't care. *Let them look.*

When the girls finally peeled apart, Tiffany's cheeks were flushed pink, her eyes shining. She turned to Ethan, still grinning.

"Dad, I told everyone my sister was visiting," she said, breathless.

"And?" he asked.

"And they thought it was cool." Tiffany hitched her backpack higher on her shoulder. "Ms. Barlow asked if Rosie wanted to come on the tide pools trip next week."

Rosie's eyes flew wide. "Can I?"

Ethan felt his mental calendar instantly reshuffle—flights, schedules, Bailey's work trips. "I don't think so. Rosie's flight leaves on Tuesday, and the field trip is on Thursday."

"Oh." Rosie's gaze dropped. "Yeah. I guess that's true."

"I'll miss you," Tiffany whispered.

The quiet ache of Rosie's departure settled in his chest. The girls would bounce back—kids always did—but it was a sharp reminder that their time together was borrowed, and already counting down.

To distract them, he put on a big, cheesy smile and interrupted them. "Who's ready for a craft?"

"We are!" Hollered Rosie.

"I am!" Copied Tiffany.

"Okay, we'd better get to the library then." He looked around at the kids loitering along the sidewalk in front of the school. "We better be ready when everyone shows up."

The afternoon sun slanted across the reading rug of the Lowell Elementary library, and a sign on the door announced: CRAFT CLUB—BRACELETS TODAY!

Below it, in firm block letters: NO GLITTER.

Ethan nodded at the sign. "Fair."

"Dad, we're late for being early," Rosie said, already moving.

The librarian, Ms. Nguyen—black bob, cardigan with little pencils embroidered on the pockets—greeted them at the counter with visible relief. "Tiffany! Hi, this must be your father—"

"And my sister!" Tiffany blurted as Ethan reached to shake her hand.

"Mr. Moore. Thanks for helping."

"I brought snacks," he said, offering a tote with apple slices and pretzel rods. He'd slapped a piece of masking tape on the lid and scrawled nut-free.

"Bless you," Ms. Nguyen said, stacking it beside the hand sanitizer. "We've got twelve set up at the tables. Elastic cord, kid scissors, tape, bowls of beads sorted by color. If you don't mind, please lead a quick clean-up at the end."

"Copy that," Ethan said.

Rosie surveyed the room like a foreman. "Okay. Tiffany, you're in charge of beads. I'll handle string." She pointed at Ethan. "You're in charge of runaways."

"Children?" he said, looking horrified.

"Beads," she said, rolling her eyes.

Tiffany drifted to the head table, fingers light on the elastic spools. She taped an end to the table, checked the stretch, and nodded to herself. Confident. Calm. Rowan's kid.

"Hi, everyone," Rosie called, big voice for a small person. Twelve heads swiveled. "We're making bracelets. Tape one end to keep your beads from escaping. Then pick a pattern—two small, one big, or rainbow. No wrong answers."

"What if they already escaped?" a boy asked.

"I'll help in a minute." Tiffany lifted her hand.

Ethan started handing out cords. His first three were too short. A boy named Caleb—gap-toothed, honest—held one up. "This won't fit a wrist."

"Oh. Yep. That one's on me," Ethan said, grabbing another length and cutting extra to compensate.

Across the table, Tiffany guided a little hand through the first few beads. "Closer pinch," she coached. "Like this."

A chorus rose—*oh no, wait, look!*—and then the sound Ethan feared: the patter of seed beads across laminate.

Ms. Nguyen closed her eyes for a beat. Ethan clapped once. "Bead Rescue Team, report." He dropped to his knees, and half the table followed. "One point for every bead you catch. Two if they don't end up down the vent."

"Make it three," Ms. Nguyen said, already scraping beads into her palm with a ruler.

"Three," Ethan agreed, sliding piles onto paper plates.

Back at the tables, Tiffany lined a larger bead near a knot. "This hides it," she told a girl named Noor. "Cheater bead. My Mom uses them."

"Your mom is the jewelry lady," Noor said reverently.

"Yeah," Tiffany said, as if it were both ordinary and enormous. "She's good at making things."

"Like you," Noor said.

Tiffany's chin tipped—just a hair, but Ethan saw it. Pride settled where worry usually sat.

At the far end, a smaller kid wrestled with a string that refused to cooperate. His mouth pulled down, eyes bright for reasons that had nothing to do with beads.

Ethan slid in beside him. "Hard day?"

The kid scowled at his hands. "My fingers are dumb."

"They're just learning," Ethan said. "Mine mess up, too. Want to trade jobs? You pass me beads, and I'll string."

The kid considered, then nodded. "But I pick the colors."

"Strong terms. Approved."

They built a simple pattern—yellow, red, red, blue—and the boy's shoulders eased. When it was time to tie, panic flickered again. Tiffany appeared at Ethan's elbow.

"Hold tight," she said, setting her own fingers over his. "One, two, pull. Not too hard or it snaps." She slid a larger bead over the knot. "Done."

Ms. Nguyen raised the library stamp. "Ten-minute warning."

Cleanup went faster than Ethan expected. He made it a game: colored bowls stacked by hue, cords rolled like snakes, tape peeled without gooey bits left behind. Rosie bossed with charm, Tiffany sorted with precision, and beads found their way home.

Kids compared wrists, shining. Noor leaned over to Tiffany. "Who did you make yours for?"

"My Mom," Tiffany said, knotting carefully, tongue tip peeking between her teeth. She chose subtle colors—smoky gray, a soft blue, a single gold bead like a sun. "She hates pink."

"Mine's for my grandma," Noor said. "She cries about everything. This will make her cry twice."

Ms. Nguyen handed Ethan the sign-out sheet and slid him a look over the top. "You were very helpful," she said. "Come back anytime."

"We will," he said—and knew he meant it.

Chapter Fourteen

Ethan

They climbed into the car at sunset. Ethan's knees ached, a dull reminder that came after an afternoon spent on kid-height chairs and library floors.

Both girls slid into the back seat without thinking, knees knocking as they buckled. Tiffany launched into a rapid recap—the spelling quiz she aced, the boy who tried to trade his pudding for her fruit snacks, the mystery meat at lunch nobody touched. Rosie listened as if it were the best story she'd heard all week, nodding in all the right spots.

His phone buzzed in the console.

He glanced down at the screen before shifting into gear.

Rowan: *Discharge planning went well. If everything stays boring, I should be home tomorrow.*

Relief moved through him slowly and deeply. He typed back one-handed.

We'll be ready.

He cleared his throat. "Hey. I just heard from Rowan."

Both heads lifted in the mirror.

"They're planning to send her home tomorrow."

For half a second, there was only blinking. Then—

"Tomorrow?" Tiffany breathed.

Rosie grinned first. "Like...actually home?"

"Actually, home," he said.

Tiffany made a small, soundless bounce in her seat. "We should do something."

In the rearview mirror, he caught their heads bending together, hands already moving, voices overlapping in that easy way siblings build a language. He'd missed this with Rosie—settling for late calls, short visits, and telling himself work mattered more.

It hadn't. This did.

"Dad?" Tiffany tugged him back.

"Yeah?"

"Can we go home and make a banner? I think there's a poster board in the closet."

Rosie perked up. "And the good markers. The ones that don't bleed."

"And glitter glue," Tiffany added, wary but hopeful. "Only a little, so mom won't get upset."

"Your mom will understand. Sparkles are important." Rosie said, grinning.

He steered toward home. "Banner it is."

They were through the door before he'd taken off his shoes, the townhouse holding that warm late-day light that made everything look softer.

From the hall closet, they unearthed a stash of craft supplies: a roll of white poster board, an old shoebox of stickers, ribbon from Rowan's projects, a dented tub of glue, and a pack of markers with more lives than they should have had.

"Mom doesn't like pink, so we'll use teal and gold," Rosie decided. "Taylor would approve."

"If Serenity's reigning fashion queen approves," Ethan said solemnly, "so do I."

They spread everything over the coffee table. Rosie took charge of layout, sketching WELCOME HOME MOM in pencil and leaving space "for flair." Tiffany worked with careful focus, tongue peeking out as she traced the first bold letter.

"Dad?" She held up a sheet of glitter alphabet stickers she'd found in a drawer. "Can we use these? So the letters are special."

He looked at her hopeful face, then at Rosie, who was already nodding. "Special letters," he said. "For your mom."

"For our mom," Tiffany corrected, soft but sure.

Rosie's hand found Tiffany's without fanfare. He swallowed past the tightness in his throat and handed over the sheet.

They settled into a rhythm: pencils scratching, tape snapping, stickers applied. The lamp cast a warm pool across the table. Fig hopped up, sniffed the glue, and, apparently approving, took up a position on the couch to supervise.

"We need a schedule," Rosie said, still writing. "So we're ready when she gets home."

"Good idea," Ethan said.

She printed in block letters on a torn sheet of paper:

Tonight: Banner.

Friday: Best Day! Mom comes home! Birthday Party!

Saturday & Sunday: Mom RESTS.

"Perfect," Tiffany said, and dotted the i in 'Birthday' with a gold sticker star.

When the banner was finished—letters bright and clean, ribbon clipped, a dusting of glitter catching the light—they taped it carefully to the wall above the couch. The townhouse, which had felt a little borrowed when he'd first arrived, looked lived-in now.

Dinner was simple—some leftover soup from Kim's warmed on the stove, toast, and apple slices fanned on a plate "because presentation mattered."

They ate cross-legged at the table, knees bumping, voices overlapping again as they told stories that made the day feel full.

Bedtime went without a fight. Toothbrushing for "two minutes, no cheating," pajamas, Shimmer Star tucked under Tiffany's chin, Rosie testing the cot and declaring it "still bouncy in a good way."

"Goodnight, Dad," Tiffany said.

"Goodnight, Dad," Rosie echoed, already half-asleep.

He stood in the doorway for a long minute, watching their breathing settle, the small rise and fall that had nothing to do with him and somehow everything to do with him now. His phone buzzed in his pocket—another meeting, another urgency from a different life.

He silenced it and slid the phone away.

In the kitchen, he added one more line to the schedule on the fridge—*Be Here*—and turned off the light.

Fig jumped onto the back of the couch and fixed him with those unblinking green eyes.

"We've got this," he said, and meant it.

Chapter Fifteen

Rowan

He could barely contain the girls as the elevator doors slid open onto the third floor, spilling them into fluorescent light and soft shoe squeaks.

"Mom gets to come home!" Tiffany squeezed his hand tighter.

"Finally." Rosie agreed.

Nurse Kelly, in a pink fox-print scrub top, spotted them and stepped forward, tablet tucked in the crook of her arm, smile quick and kind.

"Mr. Moore," she said, recognizing Ethan first. Then her gaze moved to the girls, curious and warm. "And you must be the crew I've been hearing about. I'm Kelly—your mom's lead nurse. Welcome to 3-East."

Rosie lifted her chin and smiled before offering a confident greeting, "It's a pleasure to meet you, Ms. Kelly."

Tiffany edged a half step closer to Ethan and said, "Hello."

"Are we still good to go?" Ethan asked because he knew the

difference between optimism and an actual discharge.

"Yup," Kelly said, pleased to deliver the win. "Paperwork's printing. I'll go over medication and what comes next. Ten minutes—" her mouth tipped, "—maybe a little longer."

"We're happy to wait," he said.

"We are!" chimed Rosie, as Tiffany nodded like a bobble-head doll.

"Perfect," she replied, amused, and tipped her chin toward the open door down the hall. "She's ready for you."

Rowan sat propped against pillows. The bright scarf holding back her hair brought out the color creeping back into her cheeks. She wore the same baggy shirt and loose sweats she'd worn to the hospital almost a week before. Her eyes went straight to Tiffany, then to Rosie, then settled on Ethan.

"You brought both of them," she said, something warm threading through the words and pulling tight.

"We're the Welcome Committee," Rosie declared, stepping forward with her clipboard. It was really a cutting board with a binder clip, but it made her happy. "Do you need to sign stuff so we can leave?"

"I might!" Rowan smiled. "Let's see what Kelly brings," she said.

As the girls edged closer, talking over each other, Ethan moved nearer to Rowan's side.

"I picked Tiffany up a little early," he said quietly. "Just the last bit of the day. I didn't want her to worry about pick-up or...missing this. I hope that was okay."

Her gaze flicked to his—not sharp, not angry. Just surprised.

She looked back at Tiffany, at the way she hovered on the edge of the bed, hope written all over her face.

"I'm really glad she's here," Rowan said, reaching for her. "We'll figure out how to do this parenting thing together."

He nodded once.

Rowan turned fully to Tiffany and opened her arms. "Come here, sweet girl."

Tiffany climbed onto the bed and pressed a small gift into Rowan's palm. Rainbow beads glinted on a stretchy cord.

"It's for you," she said, suddenly shy. "Because the colors are better when they're all together."

Rowan's mouth trembled. She slid the bracelet over her wrist and lifted it to study the beads more closely. "It's perfect."

Tiffany darted a look at Rosie, then back to Rowan. "Rosie says we can have matching hair for the party, so people know we're sisters."

The word landed. *Sister.* It loosened something Rowan had been holding tight since the ER. Pride and fear moved through her at once—hope, too. Across the bed, Ethan's hand settled a little firmer on the rail and then gentled, as if he'd heard the same promise.

Kelly breezed back in with a stack of papers and a plastic bag filled with small orange bottles. "Okay, team. Pain meds here. Antibiotics here. Stool softener because everyone poops. Follow up with Dr. Cole next week. No lifting more than a gallon of milk. No stairs without help. Call if the incision looks red, hot, or starts draining anything that looks gross."

Ethan was already pulling his phone out, opening the Notes app like a reflex. "How many stairs are too many stairs?

What's 'help' look like? Are we talking arm to arm, or a hand on the rail and someone spotting? Shower tomorrow? Do we need to cover the incision? How long on the antibiotic?"

Kelly's grin tilted. "I love a man with questions," she said. "Tomorrow for a shower if she feels steady. Pat dry. No scrubbing. Hairdryer on low to keep it dry. Cover if it feels better. Seven days of antibiotics. Twelve stairs is enough stairs."

He nodded and typed, thumbs quick. "No driving. No grocery runs. No lifting in general."

"No pretending to be fine," Kelly added, voice pointed, eyes on Rowan.

Rowan raised both palms. "I hear you."

"She hears me the way my son hears 'go to bed,'" Kelly muttered, but she reached over and squeezed Rowan's bare shoulder, fingers gentle at the curve of bone. "You're going home, and, no offense, I don't want to see you back here again."

Ethan slid his phone into his pocket and shifted his stance closer to the bed. "Ready, partner?" he asked, so only she could hear.

She set her jaw, bracing for something harder than a hallway stroll, and lifted the blanket. "Ready."

Sitting went fine. Standing didn't. On the second step, the floor turned to water, and color slid around the edges. She grabbed for the bed rail.

Ethan was there, hands steady at her waist, pulling her in and holding her until the spin eased and the room came back into focus. He smelled of coffee and soap. His palm found the jut of her hip without rushing it. The hand at her waist was a weight she hadn't known she'd been missing.

"Okay?" he asked, low.

"Okay," Rowan said, because it would take more than pride to ruin this.

Kelly had already swung a wheelchair into place and locked the brakes. "No heroes here," she said with a grin. "Just a pivot and sit. We'll take care of the rest."

She flipped the footrests up and set a folded blanket across the seat. "On three," she coached, one hand at Rowan's elbow, the other hovering near her shoulder. "Small steps. Turn toward the chair. Sit when you feel it behind your knees."

Rosie watched from the foot of the bed, eyes wide, filing something away with the seriousness of a child who'd learned what mattered before she could name it. Tiffany stood on tiptoe, hands fisted at her sides, ready to help but not knowing how.

"One, two, three."

Rowan turned. Ethan stayed with her, solid at her side, steady as she lowered herself into the chair. The cushions caught her. The world steadied.

Kelly dropped the footrests, guided Rowan's feet into place, and draped the blanket over her lap. "I'm putting the meds here," she said as she hung the bag on the wheelchair handle.

Ethan nodded. "Got it."

"Wait!" Tiffany halted their exit. "We almost forgot Sushi."

"Thanks, hun." Rowan lifted her arm as Tiffany tucked the pink octopus under her elbow and then looked up at Kelly. "Now, I think we're set."

"Okay. Ready for your parade?" Kelly asked.

They rolled into the hallway with Kelly at the handles. The charge nurse waved from the desk as if they were celebrities. In the elevator, Rowan's knee bumped Ethan's, and he left his hand where she could find it. The doors slid open to the lobby's bright hum, and the sliding doors sighed them out into cool air.

"Curbside," Kelly said. "I'll wait with you. You bring the car."

Ethan jogged toward the entrance lane. Rosie and Tiffany flanked the wheelchair like pint-sized security.

When he pulled up, Kelly set the chair at an angle and locked the brakes again.

"Same deal," she told Rowan. "No twisting. Scoot to the edge. One, two, three—turn and sit."

Ethan was there to take her weight. He eased her down, then adjusted the seat so it reclined just enough. Nurse Kelly tucked the blanket back over Rowan's knees and settled the seat belt low across her hips.

She handed Ethan the discharge packet and tapped the top page. "Follow-up next week. Dates on the paperwork. Numbers on the front. You're doing fine."

Rowan looked up at her. "Thank you."

Kelly's grin softened. "Now, go home."

She gave the chair a gentle kick to pivot it back toward the automatic doors and raised a hand to the girls. "Make sure you aren't back here anytime soon!"

Chapter Sixteen

Rowan

Ethan closed Rowan's door and circled to the driver's side. Rosie buckled in, holding the paperwork on her lap. Tiffany hugged Sushi and leaned forward to see her mom. Rowan let her head rest back against the seat, breath steadying as the car slid into gear.

"Okay," Tiffany announced from the backseat. "We go home, rest for twenty minutes, fix our hair, and then leave for Lily's party at four. We need socks."

With a glance in the rearview mirror, Ethan laughed. "We won't forget the socks."

"The birthday party?" Rowan asked, careful with her turn.

Ethan glanced at her pale face in the passenger seat. "Forget?"

"Yeah, I was just excited to come home, I guess." Rowan's brows pulled together. "Are you sure it's not too much?"

"Rosie's schedule aside, I have a plan for today. I'm not making the girls miss a party with their friends because I can't juggle. We'll get you on the couch, pillows like a throne. They'll jump and eat cake, and I'll bring them back in one piece."

She looked up at the thin blue strip of sky between the clouds. For so long, the breaking and fixing had been hers alone. He said we, and she believed him. "Okay," she said. "Go have cake."

Tiffany let out a breath. "Dad says we're a team. Your job is resting. Our job is to be kids."

"Mission approved," Rosie added, tapping her mock clipboard.

The townhouse door opened on teal-and-gold letters that shouted WELCOME HOME MOM across the wall, glitter catching the light. Flowers brightened a mason jar on the kitchen counter. A list on the fridge—boxes, times, a thick underline on library books—ended with a square note in block print: *Be Here.*

Rowan stepped in and felt the air shift. The sink wasn't empty. A blanket fort slouched near the couch. A comet-tail of dried paint marked the coffee table. The fridge hummed as Ethan tucked the pharmacy bag in. Leftover spaghetti, rotisserie chicken, and cut fruit in clear tubs—three kinds of kids' yogurt. Post-Its dotted the door. *Rosie 8 p.m. ?? ASK B.*

Objectively, it wasn't tidy, but the girls glowed as if they'd swallowed small suns.

Ethan had the couch ready for her—pillows, a blanket, the right angle to keep the pull from catching under her ribs. He helped her get settled and slid a rolled towel beneath her knees.

He pointed at the couch. "Sit. Rest." He set the remote and her water within reach. "Ten minutes to get them party-ready."

Rosie placed a yellow gift bag with rainbow wrapping tissue on the kitchen table. The printed tag hanging from the bag read 'LILY' in neat block letters. "Almost ready," she said and disappeared down the hall. Tiffany hovered, feet restless.

"Come here," Rowan said, crooking a finger. She tucked a stray hair behind Tiffany's ear and tried not to notice how much taller she seemed after six days. "Excited?"

"A lot," Tiffany said, then added, "I can skip if you want me to stay."

"If you skip a trampoline party," Rowan deadpanned, "I'll be very disappointed."

Relief flashed. "Rosie says she can do fancy buns but sturdy, like the Olympics."

"You'll need bobby pins," Rowan called.

"Got 'em," Rosie answered, voice all business. "And hairspray."

They set up in the hallway mirror. Rosie stood behind Tiffany, brows down, tongue caught in concentration as she anchored two tight buns as if she expected crosswinds. In the glass, one face was grave, one pleased. Rowan's throat tightened.

At the coffee table, Ethan sat down to sort Rowan's medication and make a dosage list. He glanced up, caught the shine in Rowan's eyes, and stayed quiet.

Tiffany appeared in the doorway in party shoes, holding a little tension in her shoulders. "You're *really* okay if we go?"

"Baby, of course," Rowan said. "Go have cake. Bring me home a story."

"Two stories," Rosie promised. "I wonder if they'll have a laser light show."

"We're going to a trampoline park, not a rave," Ethan said, smiling.

Tiffany darted back to kiss Rowan's cheek. "I'll text you if the cake is weird."

"Do," Rowan said.

Gift. Socks. Keys. Ethan helped with Tiffany's jacket and waited for the small tilt of her chin so he could zip it like always. At the door, he met Rowan's gaze.

"Call if you need me."

"I will." She rolled her eyes so she wouldn't cry.

The door clicked shut on their familiar sounds. The quiet settled around her. She was grateful for the absence of hospital sounds. Rowan eased back into the pillows he'd arranged and lifted her wrist. The rainbow beads warmed against her skin, catching the light.

Home, she thought, and let the word sink in.

Chapter Seventeen

Ethan

The trampoline park was in a squat, gray concrete block building between a tire shop and a nail salon. It looked unremarkable from the street, but it was pure chaos once you stepped inside. The air smelled of rubber and sugar. Music thumped. Fluorescent lines streaked the floor like highlighter marks.

"Shoes off," Rosie announced the second they cleared the threshold, already untying her sneakers and hopping on one foot. "We need grip socks and the paper things."

Ethan eyed a wall covered in clipboards and felt his blood pressure twitch. "Come on," he told the attendant, "let me sign my soul away."

"Three jumpers?" the teenager behind the counter asked, popping a piece of gum and sliding their signed release forms across the desk. "Birthday party room is in the back. Table with pink balloons."

"Two jumpers," Ethan corrected, glancing at the sea of trampolines beyond the glass. "One...emotional support adult."

Tiffany slipped her hand through his elbow without looking like she meant to. "You said you'd jump if I got nervous."

"I did," he said, squaring up to the reality of that promise. "Three jumpers, please."

They found Lily first—freckled, gap-toothed, with a sparkly headband holding back flyaway blonde hair. She stood behind a tower of gift bags like a reigning queen.

"Happy birthday," Tiffany said, shy but direct, holding out their carefully wrapped gift bag with both hands. "It's...art stuff. The fancy kind."

Lily's face split wide. "This is the best." She hugged Tiffany like she meant it and then flung an arm around Rosie on principle. "Come bounce!"

A whistle blew near the foam pit. A teenager in a polo and earnest expression climbed onto a platform and launched into a safety briefing about "knees bent," "one at a time," and "no flips unless you can stick the landing." Kids stared at him as if he were speaking a foreign language. Parents hovered in a clump near the party room door, already angling for outlets and caffeine.

Tiffany slid her palm down Ethan's sleeve, a tiny stroke he felt all the way to his backbone. "You're going to do it, right?"

"I'm going to do it," he said.

They started small—open jump, the long field of blue and black squares that lifted and dropped with every step. Rosie took to it like she'd been born mid-air, ponytail flying, knees hitting the sweet spot between reckless and athletic. Tiffany bounced once, twice, testing the give, orbs of concentration deep in her eyes.

"You've got this," Ethan said.

She nodded, then lifted and landed. Lifted, landed. Caution loosened into rhythm. The music drowned out the rubbery thump of bodies turning gravity into a suggestion. When she hit a clean, high note, she barked a laugh, startled and delighted in the same breath.

"Look at you," he said, proud enough to make his chest ache.

"Your turn," she said, deadpan.

He stepped onto the mat. The world went springy. A staff kid in a polo shirt drifted past with the look of someone about to witness something he'd talk about at dinner.

"Don't overthink it," Rosie called.

Overthink it? He survived on overthinking.

He crouched, pushed, and felt the trampoline give back. Up. Down. Up—arms out without thought, legs depending on old instincts, and getting very little help from actual skill. He tried a twist. His arms windmilled.

"Dad," Rosie yelled, delighted. "You look like the octopus at the aquarium."

"Thank you," he said, mid-bounce, his dignity shedding like loose change.

"Bend your knees," Tiffany ordered, bossy now that she was sure her dad was keeping his promises. "You're making it harder."

He bent. It helped. It also made him look more like a startled giraffe. He landed, breathless and sputtering, receiving the feral applause only nine-year-olds can give.

"Goated," Rosie declared. "Fully lit."

"I aspire to adequacy," he said, chasing air with a grin.

They ping-ponged between dodgeball, the foam pit (float, sink, shriek, repeat), and the balance beam over a vat of mangled foam cubes. Every time the noise rose around her, Tiffany sought him out with her eyes. Every time he was near, her hand lifted, palm open.

The moms found him near the vending machines, red from effort, sucking down water.

"You're a dad?" one asked, friendly and curious, and already knowing the answer.

"Tiffany's," he said.

She smiled, a curious light in her eyes, then tipped her head toward the party room where a group of women was laughing so hard one had hooked an arm over the back of a chair for support. "You can sit with us. We're talking about the toddler who flushed her shoe."

"What kind of shoe?" he asked before his brain could stop his mouth. "Sneaker? Ballet flat? There are so many implications—"

The moms blinked.

He glanced down at his cup. "You know what—ignore me. I'm new."

He tried again later, after the whistles signaled a shift from chaos to sugar. He slid into the edge of their circle with the ingratiating smile of a man who knew how to enter a boardroom.

"Make a wish!" someone trilled. Lily beamed. The candles guttered. A roar of tiny voices drowned out the music. Rosie led an off-key chorus with the gusto of a general. Tiffany clapped a beat late on purpose, newly minted mischief.

"So," he ventured, "how is everyone handling the drop-off system? It seems like we could fix the flow if—"

"We were still talking about having kids," another mom said kindly. "And how none of us have recovered."

"Right," he said. They stared at him for a beat too long. Somewhere behind him, one of his children cackled. He excused himself to find napkins and what remained of his dignity at another table.

"Excuse me!" someone called. A harried twenty-something with a paper hat and a knife was wrestling a block of ice cream cake that was being difficult. "Help?"

He stepped in, took the cake knife, and felt curiosity ripple across the mom table. The cake was as hard as a rock. He buried the blade, leaned on it as though it owed him money, and carved out a clean slab. The room hummed with respect now. One woman fanned herself with a paper plate as if she'd just witnessed a genuine hero at work.

"Do you want individual plating," he asked, checking his spacing, "or should we set up an...equal-distribution plan?"

"Plates, please," the party mom said, trying not to laugh. "You're hired."

He cut, served, plated, and handed over slices like he was moving through a tasting line—first the kids, then the adults, the knife sliding just enough to keep momentum. Someone behind him murmured, "and those arms," and he chose gratitude over mortification.

Another mom raised a brow and mouthed, *Available?*

The flicker of panic took him straight back to his youth, and he answered before he could overthink it. "I'm... committed." He nodded toward the girls.

He saw the understanding click into place and felt himself relax.

When the sugar hit, the room reached a pitch that felt like it might crack glass.

Ethan leaned against the door frame and watched both girls sit shoulder to shoulder with Lily, heads bent over party favors. Their bun crowns had shifted—Rosie's was still defiant, Tiffany's softening into a lop-sided halo. They looked exactly like what Rowan had wanted for them without saying it out loud: *a hot mess and a tight unit.*

He boxed up a cupcake, asked for an extra napkin, and tucked it into the crook of his arm. On the way out, he located shoes that had migrated to unlikely places, signed a stray birthday card with a heart the size of a dime when Lily shoved it at him with a pen, and collected two crinkly goodie bags.

In the parking lot, twilight had tipped the sky toward lavender. Rosie marched ahead, but Tiffany stayed close, fingers hooked in his sleeve. They buckled in without being asked. He glanced in the rearview mirror and caught the heart-shaped mirror of two heads leaning toward each other as they compared trinkets.

"Cake verdict?" he asked, easing the car into gear.

"Fudge layer was too cold," Rosie declared.

"Sprinkles were on theme," Tiffany said. "I'm glad they had cupcakes too, for the dairy-free friends. You got one for Mom?" she added automatically, then caught herself and smiled. "We'll say it's from you."

"I know she would have loved to be there," he said, but he kept the rest to himself. *He would have loved for her to be there.* It wasn't the other moms he wanted ogling him, and they certainly weren't the ones he was trying to impress.

Traffic thinned. The car warmed. The party noise faded, leaving them with the soft shuffle of paper bags. At a red light, he reached back and touched Tiffany's ankle through her sock—a small check-in. She didn't startle. She squeezed his fingers with hers, then let go.

They turned onto Rowan's street. Porch lights flickered on up and down the block. He pulled into the space by the townhouse and cut the engine. For a second, the quiet hung—anticipation, gratitude, a small stretch of relief.

"Cupcake?" Rosie reminded him, practical even now.

He lifted the white box. "Check."

Tiffany reached for the door handle and paused, looking at the second-floor window. "Do you think she fell asleep?"

He pictured Rowan on the couch, pillows like a throne, teal-and-gold banner lifting when the heater kicked on.

"If she did," he said, "we'll be careful not to wake her up."

He balanced the box, grabbed the keys, and followed the girls up the stairs. He slid the key into the lock, heard the faint thump of Fig dismounting from her perch on the windowsill, and he smiled at the thought of their domestic bliss.

Chapter Eighteen

Rowan

Rowan sat motionless, letting the familiar rhythm of home wash over her. Everything here should look the same, sound the same, but an entire part of her life had slipped out of reach, and she could feel the shape of its absence.

The townhouse carried a quiet hum she hadn't noticed in years—the steady churn of the refrigerator, the hallway heater clicking on, the faint tap of rain against the window. Threaded beneath those familiar sounds was the echo of the week she'd missed, a tune she could almost catch if she closed her eyes: Tiffany's laugh drifting from the kitchen, the dry whisper of markers on poster board while Ethan tried his hand at being the one who kept everything running, the clatter of pans as someone else made dinner in her place.

She eased to the edge of the couch and studied the welcome-home touches, the evidence of the week she'd missed unfolding in small, bright details.

The banner on the living room wall shimmered with tiny

teal sparkles every time the air vent kicked on. Flowers crowded the counter in a mismatched mason jar, stems fanned out, daisies tilting their sunny faces toward the window. A list on the fridge mapped out their days in uneven handwriting, and at the bottom, a single crooked sticker proclaimed *GOOD JOB* in shiny rainbow letters.

The smile came easily. She could almost see Tiffany pressing that sticker into place, a small vote of confidence for Ethan.

Rowan let her fingers drift over the couch cushion where Ethan had sprawled the night before, aware of how much her place had changed in a week—and none of it because of new throw pillows. She'd lived by her own rhythm for so long that quiet had become something hard-won in the constant negotiation of life and caregiving. But this lack of demand created a different sort of stillness. It didn't echo. It made room.

There wasn't much she *could* do yet, and, for a change, there was nothing she *needed* to do.

Her thoughts unwound on their own, steady and unstoppable:

Ethan at her bedside, asking the right questions. His hand resting over hers, warm and steady. His voice pitched low when he said, "You called. I came."

Tiffany leaning against him at the aquarium.

Rosie appointed herself big sister without hesitation.

Both girls saying 'Dad' today as if the word had always belonged to him.

The memories pressed forward, faster than she could manage, just beginning to outpace her control until Fig materialized from whatever hiding place she'd chosen for her dramatic entrance.

The gray puff launched herself onto the arm of the couch, tail swishing, her green eyes bright with judgment and curiosity. Rowan lifted her good hand and scratched under her chin.

"You survived," she murmured. "Me too."

Snuggled against the cat, she drifted in and out. The couch warmed beneath her, and the room settled into a slow, unhurried tick of the clock. She came awake when the townhouse shifted around her. The air changed in that subtle way it does when weather moves, or someone steps through the door.

Then came the sounds she'd been waiting for: the scuff of sneakers in the hall, Rosie's bright burst of laughter, and Tiffany's breathless reply tumbling right after it. Behind them, Ethan's voice was deeper, steadier. The low tone was becoming familiar all over again.

"Mom!" Tiffany's shoes squeaked as she launched herself forward and then stopped short, remembering. Careful hands landed on Rowan's arm and shoulder, light but sure. "We brought you a cupcake and a story!"

"Lots of stories," Rosie corrected, already taking off her jacket and flinging it across the back of a chair with a flourish that promised drama.

Ethan slipped inside, locked the door, and set his keys in the dish on the front table like he'd been doing it for years. His hair was a little wild.

"How was it?" Rowan asked, bracing herself for the onslaught.

Rosie placed a hand on her hip. "Dad tried to talk to the moms."

Ethan made a small sound that suggested he wished he were anywhere else.

"He walked up to their table," Rosie continued, voice perfectly flat, "and said, 'So...is anyone else struggling to adjust to the new drop-off routine?'"

Ethan winced. "It was a reasonable question."

"They weren't talking about school stuff," Rosie said. "They were talking about a toddler who flushed a shoe down the toilet. A *shoe*, Dad. They were laughing so hard that one of them was crying."

"I didn't know the topic," Ethan protested, palms lifted in defeat. "I was trying to join in."

"They all just kind of...stared," Rosie said, widening her eyes for effect. "He was so awkward."

"I was attempting to make conversation," Ethan said, resigned.

"You attempted something," Rosie agreed. "Oh! And the trampoline!"

Tiffany took over, hands lifting as if sculpting the memory in midair. "He promised he would jump with me if I got nervous. Then he went on and tried to do a twirl turn and his arms—" she sucked in a breath sharp enough to whistle and flung her limbs out like a startled creature, "—went everywhere. Like the octopus at the aquarium swallowed a person."

Rosie collapsed onto the rug in dramatic appreciation. "It was unhinged. 10/10."

"I was participating," Ethan said, though the corner of his mouth betrayed him.

"And then," Tiffany continued, eyes going wide, "when the

moms needed someone to cut the ice cream cake because the knife got stuck, Dad took it and said—"

Rosie popped up on one elbow. "He said, 'Should I plate and serve, or is there a distribution plan?' He said it like that was a normal thing anyone at a children's trampoline park would say."

"They thanked me," Ethan insisted. "I was a hero."

"They thanked you because you used your big arms to cut cake," Rosie said. "Hero's a stretch."

"Big arms," Tiffany repeated, solemn.

Rowan couldn't stop smiling. She was sore and frayed from the week, yet the part of her that always held joy at arm's length loosened, letting it settle close to her heart.

"Did you have fun?" she asked Tiffany, cutting through the teasing, needing the answer from the only witness who mattered.

Tiffany nodded so hard her buns wobbled. "We jumped, and I didn't hide when the kids were loud. I wanted to a little, and then I remembered Rosie said she'd come back and handle it if anyone was rude, and it felt like it was okay to be there."

"That's my brave girl," Rowan said, throat tightening.

"She *was* brave," Rosie agreed, bumping her shoulder gently into Tiffany's. Tiffany leaned back, a soft lean that wasn't showy. They sat like that for a beat, a new shape Rowan could have stared at for hours.

"Dinner, then bath, then two chapters, because it's already late for the T Team."

"T Team?" Rowan echoed, smiling.

Rosie pointed proudly at the fridge. "Tomorrow's your rest

day. We're helpers. The 'Take Care of Mom Team.'"

Rowan followed her gesture to the list and read:

Saturday & Sunday: Mom RESTS.

Big block letters with hearts framing the word *rests*.

Tiffany appeared at her side with a small white bakery box, wearing a seriousness that tugged hard at Rowan's heart. "We brought you one that didn't have too much frosting," she said. "'Cause you don't like when the top is taller than the bottom."

"Give me a hug," Rowan murmured. Tiffany leaned in, and Rowan kissed her forehead. "Thank you for knowing me."

They ate dinner on the couch, the four of them pressed in close around the coffee table. Afterward, they laughed and watched Rowan take her first bite of the cupcake. Vanilla frosting, sweet and balanced. Soft cake. Crumbs worth chasing with a fingertip.

"Brush and baths," Ethan announced once the last napkin had been balled and tossed. "Dirty clothes and shoes away. Don't pretend to forget."

Rosie sighed and disappeared down the hall with Tiffany at her side. Fig abandoned her post by the living room window and followed in their wake, tail high.

"Are you okay?" Ethan asked when they were alone in the living room. He was still standing, hands on his hips, prepared to spring into action at any moment.

"I'm better," she said. "Tired. Happy."

She watched the tension ease out of his shoulders at that last word. She could tell he'd been bracing for something else entirely.

He scrubbed a hand over his jaw, color rising just enough to catch her notice. "For the record, I did *not* expect to be the only dad at that party. The moms kept thanking me for...my arms."

Rowan lifted a brow. "Your cake-cutting arms?"

He groaned. "Yes. Apparently, that's a thing now."

"Well," she said lightly, "you *did* slice through an ice-cream cake. I've heard that can be quite difficult."

"That was practicality," he insisted. "The knife was stuck on the fudge."

"Mm-hmm."

"I did more than cut," he added, warming to the joke. "I also carried and opened things."

"Sure." She let herself smile, a little too pleased at the idea of all those moms noticing him. "Sounds like you made an impression."

"An unfortunate one," he muttered. "One woman asked if I was 'available for future events.' I think she meant cake duty, but I panicked and said I was currently...committed."

Her pulse hitched. "Committed?"

"To the team," he said quickly, nodding toward the fridge where the 'Take Care of Mom Team' list hung. "And to keeping everyone alive this week. That felt like enough."

His laugh escaped then, low and mostly breath. He bent to gather the discarded tissues and the cupcake box, moving through her kitchen with the quiet ease of someone who knew where everything lived now: the trash under the sink, the drawer that stuck unless you tugged it just right, and the utensils in the drawer to the right of the stove.

It was such an ordinary thing, but it was ordinariness that undid her. He'd been useful all week—backpack wrangler, form signer, grocery buyer, hospital visitor.

But this wasn't just usefulness. It was closer to...belonging.

The girls barreled back into the room, hair damp and pajamas mismatched in ways that made their personalities obvious. Their cheeks were flushed from warm water, their scent all lavender soap and childhood.

"Two chapters," Rosie declared, sliding onto the couch and smacking the cushion beside her. "From the bear book."

"Three," Tiffany countered, borrowing some confidence from Rosie.

"Two," Ethan repeated, good-natured, lifting the book, settling between them before reading the first line.

Rowan had never realized what a gentle gift that could be until she saw Tiffany's shoulders drop, melting into the cotton of her pajama shirt.

They laughed in the right places, got quiet when the bear tried to make a friend, and fumbled it. Rowan watched Ethan stop for questions and go back when Tiffany wanted to understand why the bear had said something. He didn't hurry. He didn't turn the lesson into a lecture. He just shared the moment with them.

After the second chapter, Rosie tipped over like a felled tree. "Fine," she said into the cushion. "You win."

Ethan walked them down the hall and returned slowly. He gathered juice pouches off the coffee table, checked the front lock again without comment, and then crossed back to the couch and sat in the space at her feet.

They looked at each other for a long beat while the townhouse breathed around them.

"You're good with them," Rowan said finally, because not saying it felt like pretending she didn't see it at all.

"I love them," he said, as if he'd been waiting to say it to her in those exact words. "I love how Rosie takes charge like the world is waiting for her to tell it what to do. I love how Tiff watches everything, takes what she needs, and then gives it back better. I love that they've claimed each other like there was never any other way this could go."

"And me?" The question was out before she could wrestle it back. It wasn't coy. It wasn't a trap. She didn't even know what answer she wanted until she heard herself ask.

"I love the way our girls are growing into strong kids because of their mothers," he said. "I hate that I didn't make that easier. I can't change what I missed, but I can change now." He didn't flinch. "You," he added, something strong and gentle threaded together in his voice. "I'm trying very hard not to steamroll the parts of you that took a long time to build. If you're asking...yes."

She let out a breath. The word yes rippled through places she'd boarded up. She didn't move, didn't reach for him. Her body ached. Her heart had learned caution, but there it was, the truth between them, simple and unadorned.

Instead of beckoning her closer, he nudged the coffee table a few inches with his knee and lowered himself to the floor beside the couch. He folded his forearms on the cushion near her knees and set his palm warm over her shin, just above the blanket's edge.

Down the hall, the girls' room went quiet in fits and starts—the thump of a book, a muffled giggle, then the soft settle of sleep. Fig reclaimed the armrest throne and watched them like she had opinions she didn't intend to share.

Rowan turned her head and studied his profile. The plane of his jaw, the little dent in his cheek he called a flaw, and she had always liked, the way his eyes softened when the world let him rest. He was a polished man and had made a life out of that polish. Tonight, he looked worn out. It suited him. It suited them.

"I thought I was going to do all of this alone," she said, voice low so it didn't ripple the moment. "And I could have kept doing it. I would have, but I don't want to anymore."

He looked at the banner, at the kitchen, at the closed door that held their girls. When he looked back, nothing in his face was for show. "Then don't," he said.

She set her hand on his wrist, thumb finding the steady beat there, a private metronome. He turned his hand, and their fingers fit the way they had in the hospital chair, like an old habit they were picking up again.

Time thinned. The couch held her. He rose only to flip off the lamp and check the lock, then came back to her side and bent to kiss her forehead the way he had before. She turned into it, not because she needed care, but because she wanted him.

"Rest," he said. "I'll be right here."

She believed him.

Later, when they had fully settled, he pushed to his feet and offered his hand. "Let me help you to bed," he said.

She nodded. He slid an arm close, not carrying, just steadying her at her elbow and the small of her back. They took the short walk in slow steps. In her room, he eased her down, fussed with pillows until the pull eased under her ribs, set water and her meds within reach, and left the door open the way she liked it.

"You're due for pain meds around 2 a.m. I'll check on you then."

From the doorway, she watched him move through the small space with quiet competence. He carried a glass to the sink, wrote a quick note on the fridge, and straightened a corner of the banner that had peeled up. Fig gave up and curled herself into a gray comma on the rug.

She watched him tidy and realized how easy this life would be. With him in it, bending with the boring things, staying for the hard ones, making two girls laugh until they tipped over.

I could fall in love with this, she thought.

Chapter Nineteen

Rowan

It might have been the tug under her ribs or the faint clink of a spoon that woke her. Pain and morning sounds braided together until Rowan opened her eyes and found the room filled with soft, slanting light.

Through the cracked door, she could see a slice of the living room and the edge of the kitchen. The teal-and-gold banner hung a little crooked where the tape had given up on one corner. Glitter winked from the rug. Cartoons murmured at a respect-ful volume.

Her body took stock. Dry mouth. A manageable ache. Hunger instead of nausea.

She swung her legs carefully over the side of the bed and tested her balance. Five slow steps to the kitchen. She wanted the mug with the chipped rim, the one from the flea market with the faded blue flowers. She wanted proof that this was still her space.

She made it two steps.

The room tilted.

"Ethan?" she called, panting.

He appeared almost immediately. Bare feet. Soft clothes. A dark dusting of stubble still covered his face.

"Hey there, it's almost time for your meds. I was just making tea." He took in her posture, her breathing. "Do you want help?"

She hated how much she did.

"Yes."

He crossed the room without rushing. "May I?"

She nodded, annoyed at how grateful her body felt at the simple question.

His hands settled at her waist—warm, steady, anchoring. They moved together, slow as tidewater, until she could lean against the counter and blink the sparks from her vision.

"Breathe with me," he murmured. "In. Two, three. Out. Two, three, four."

She did. The tightness eased. Not gone. Livable.

"Okay?" he asked.

"Okay," she said, meaning only right now.

He let go without ceremony and turned to the kettle. "Tea or mug?"

"Tea. With a small scoop of the local honey. I'm trying to be agreeable so I can negotiate a coffee after lunch."

His smile was quick. "Duly noted."

She had to admit, the domestic track suited him. Water poured against metal. The click of the stove. The soft staccato of Fig jumping down and trotting to her food dish with exaggerated dignity.

Ethan moved through her kitchen, locating the tea tin without looking, finding the honey in the cabinet over the stove because that was where she always kept it—when she remembered.

She leaned her hip against the counter and traced the groove in the laminate that ran like a river halfway to the sink. "Thanks for helping me out of bed."

"I've been up for a while," he said. "A cat was staring at me. I value my life. I had to get up and feed it."

Footsteps pattered down the hall. Rosie appeared first, hair a riot of curls, pajama pants covered in tiny rockets, clipboard tucked under her arm like she had an early staff meeting. Tiffany trailed her, hugging Shimmer Star under one arm and stretching up onto her toes to see what was happening.

"Take-Care-of-Mom Team reporting," Rosie announced. "We prepared a recovery schedule."

"You prepared a schedule," Rowan asked quizzically.

"With times," Tiffany added proudly.

Rowan laughed and opened her arms. "Come here, sweet girl."

Tiffany said, slipping her hand into Rowan's. She stood there without speaking for a while, small and steady as if the simple touch could hold everything together. When Fig rubbed against her ankle, she bent and gave the cat a solemn hello, then refocused on Rowan. "Does it hurt right now?"

"A little," Rowan said, never one for pretty lies. "It's better than yesterday."

Tiffany nodded.

They ate toast at the counter, hip to hip. Ethan read

the medication labels. Rosie set timers. Tiffany kept nudging Rowan's plate closer, as if sharing might hold the world in place.

Halfway through breakfast, a white-hot twinge caught under Rowan's ribs. It was sudden and reminded her of her body's limits. She closed her eyes and reached for the counter.

Rowan closed her eyes.

Ethan's hand was there immediately, steady at her back. "I think it's time for you to sit back down."

The girls watched quietly as he moved her back to the couch and measured out her medication.

"Better," Rowan said.

"Good."

By late morning, the couch had become Rowan's command center. Pillows adjusted to the perfect height, water within reach, remote exactly where she could grab it without twisting. The girls set out colored pencils and paper while the cat decided the coffee table was her stage.

"We should make something for Nurse Kelly," Rowan said.

Tiffany brightened at once. "Make her a fox. Her scrubs had tiny foxes. I counted them when I was nervous."

"A fox it is," Rowan said.

Ethan glanced at the supplies on the bookshelf and didn't move until she nodded. Then he brought her the small jeweler's block, a tin of stamps, the lighter hammer, and the soft cloth she wrapped her finished pieces in. He set the tray across her knees, his eyes asking a question without words. *Like this?*

"Perfect," she said. "Thanks."

Her hands remembered, even if her body insisted on breaks she wouldn't have taken a month ago. She chose a small oval of silver, pressed it beneath the stamp with care, then lifted the hammer and let it fall soft and true. The fox rose from the metal in a clean, simple outline.

The sound of the hammer was familiar as a heartbeat. Tap, lift, turn. Tap. She punched a small hole, smoothed the edge, and polished until the silver caught a kiss of light. She slid a tiny smoky quartz onto the jump ring, a stone meant for grounding and healing.

She reached into one of the small tins on the tray and drew out a bead she'd been hoarding—a sliver of polished myrtle wood, warm and glossy, its grain catching the light like liquid honey. She'd bought it from a market vendor the year before and saved it for the right person. Nurse Kelly had earned something rare.

"Pretty," Tiffany breathed, chin on the couch, eyes wide.

"For beauty and strength," Rowan said. "And calm."

"We'll need a good box." Ethan sat on the floor near her feet, quiet as a held breath. "And handwriting that does not look like mine."

"I'll write the note," Tiffany said. "Dear Ms. Kelly, thank you for taking good care of my mom. Love, Tiffany."

Ethan found a tiny velvet pouch and a small white box in the drawer where Rowan kept ribbons and spare earring backs. He slipped the pendant into the pouch and handed the paper to Rosie. She printed the note in careful block letters, then passed it to Tiffany, who added a small fox face in the corner.

"I can drop it off to Nurse Kelly after Tiffany heads to school on Monday?"

"Perfect," Rowan said, her throat tight in the best way.

Tiffany looked up and grinned. "We can put Mom's sticker on the box so she knows it's a handmade gift."

Rosie nodded. "Like her *official* stuff."

Rowan looked from the box to the banner to the two faces that had found each other like magnets. Then her gaze slid to Ethan, who was pretending to care deeply about a tuft in the carpet, and something inside her settled. Not fireworks. Not relief. A simple answer she'd wanted for longer than she was ready to admit.

"We are good," she said, half to herself and half to the room.

"Yeah," Ethan said without turning. "We are."

Lunch was an oddly triumphant bowl of tomato soup and grilled cheese that wasn't burnt, which everyone acknowledged as a major step forward for the chef.

Tiffany created an assembly line at the stove while Ethan flipped the actual sandwiches. Rosie cut the bread on the diagonal and insisted that they garnish the plates with rose-shaped carrots.

The afternoon softened. A fort happened, and a movie—with popcorn—was called for.

They settled on the floor, two girls tucked in like bookends. Ethan lowered himself to the rug beside the couch again. He stretched his hand up to where hers rested and, without looking, she slid her fingers into his. He kept them there, an easy link while the cartoon pig sang on the screen.

When the movie credits rolled, and the fort collapsed under

the weight of Fig's curiosity, Rowan blinked into the quiet room and felt something in her chest ease. She was not back to normal. She was not even sure normal was a thing to aim for anymore. But the edges of her life had softened, making room for the possibility of what could be.

Ethan stood and offered his hand. "Nap," he said

"I don't nap."

"You do today."

She took his hand because that was easier than always being brave alone.

He walked with her down the hall, slow and steady, waited while she eased into bed, set a glass of water within reach, and adjusted the shade so the light was a soft glow, not a glare. When he tucked the blanket over her knees, his fingers brushed her shin through the sheet—the lightest, briefest stroke.

It sent a little spark through her blood, showing in her smile whether she wanted it to or not.

"Careful," she murmured. "You keep that up, and we will have a different sort of problem."

His mouth quirked. "Noted, but I do have a certain sort of reputation to protect."

"No one has forgotten the power of your cake-cutting arms," she said.

He chuckled, then sobered as he bent down and pressed his mouth to her temple. The kiss was warm and steady and nothing like the hospital fluorescent kind. "Rest. We are here."

She believed him.

Chapter Twenty

Ethan

The girls were restless.

There wasn't a fort, movie, or mom-approved craft that could entertain them anymore.

It had seemed like a good idea to slip out and give Rowan some time alone while he took the girls to restock and regroup. Practical. Efficient. The sort of decision he'd always been good at making, but the Sunday Farmer's Market, clearly, had been aspirational.

He felt it the moment they stepped between the stalls. He was in over his head. This was Rowan's territory.

The air hummed—not with urgency or salesmanship, but with community instead of competition. People greeted one another by name, dogs slept under tables, and kids walked up to stalls with crinkled dollar bills and anxious-looking parents.

This wasn't a place you passed through.

It was a place where you belonged.

The air hummed with familiarity—vendors calling out

prices without looking up, regulars trading gossip along with change, names exchanged casually. He adjusted the tote on his shoulder and followed Rosie as she cut a purposeful path through the crowd, manager energy radiating off her even without her faux clipboard.

"Okay," she announced, stopping short at the apple stand. "Mom says, 'An apple a day keeps the doctor away.'"

Tiffany trailed behind him. "We also need something for dinner."

The vendors clocked him immediately.

One Dad. Two girls. One was in charge, the other was narrating, and he just looked confused.

Samples appeared as if by magic. Apple slices. Cheese cubes on toothpicks. A woman with windburned cheeks leaned down and asked Rosie what she thought of the Honeycrisps.

Rosie accepted the slice, chewed slowly, and nodded once. "Good texture," she said. "But a little sweet. Four out of five stars."

The woman beamed. "County fair judge?"

"Her mom," Ethan said.

Rosie shot him a look. "Former. Three years running."

They moved on with a bag of apples and a handful of cider donuts, Tiffany insisted were "seasonal, so we have to get them while we can." Then, at the herb stand, she buried her nose in a bunch of rosemary and inhaled like she was trying to absorb it through her sinuses.

"These will help Mom feel better," she declared. "They smell like dinner."

Ethan smiled despite himself. He added rosemary and

thyme to the tote. Bread followed—dense sourdough with a crispy, crackled crust. Bone broth made the list because Tiffany said, "Healing, duh," and Rosie nodded like that settled it.

Flowers slowed them down.

They stood in front of galvanized buckets brimming with color. Tiffany eyed a bunch of pink peonies. "No pink."

"They're too...fancy," Rosie added, as if that were a flaw.

"Orange is happy," Tiffany argued, pointing to a riot of marigolds. "And orange is also a fruit."

"White," Rosie countered. "With leaves. That looks more official."

"Official for what?" Ethan asked.

"For healing," Rosie said patiently.

"White with leaves and a sprinkle of orange," he agreed, grateful for the consensus.

His phone buzzed in his pocket. Once. Then again.

Harrison. On a Sunday.

He didn't need to look to know what it would say, but he did anyway—habit, reflex. *Thursday. Distributor deck. In-person.* The words stacked up like building blocks he'd spent years arranging his life around. *Tiffany's field trip.*

He turned the phone face down in the tote and kept walking.

"Alright, team," he said, aiming for light. "Last stop."

The jewelry booth sat near the end, rays of sunlight catching on metal and stone. The owner looked up and smiled widely when she saw Tiffany.

"Hey, you," she said. "Your mom sold out of those hammered hoops last week."

She slid a shallow dish of tumbled stones toward the girls. "Pick one for luck."

Tiffany chose a pale blue oval and closed her fist around it. Rosie selected a green one after a long deliberation.

The woman straightened and looked at Ethan while directing her question to Tiffany. "And who is on duty with you today, kiddo?"

"My Dad," she said without hesitation.

"Oh—nice to meet you," the woman said. Her eyes flicked back toward the space behind them. "Rowan's here most Sundays. Guys are always trying to chat her up. I just assumed she was single."

"Good for her," Ethan said, but felt it anyway—the tightening under his ribs, the involuntary clench of his jaw.

Rosie's gaze snapped to him, sharp and assessing.

The woman glanced at his hand, bare. "Never noticed a ring."

"It was nice to meet you," he said, already stepping away.

Tiffany slipped her stone into her pocket and hooked two fingers into his sleeve, anchoring him as they merged back into the crowd.

The walk home was quieter. The grocery tote dug into his palm. Rosie matched his stride, thoughtful.

"You didn't like that lady talking about guys flirting with Rowan," she said, careful like she was testing a hypothesis.

"It's none of my business," he replied.

"Mmm," Rosie said. The sound carried judgment and curiosity in equal measure.

Next to them, Tiffany's sneakers slapped the pavement in

an uneven rhythm, counting time.

"Support," Ethan muttered under his breath. "Help. Parent. No expectations."

His brain, traitorous, offered a montage anyway—faceless men leaning over the booth, laughing too loud, buying bracelets for reasons that had nothing to do with jewelry.

He adjusted his grip on the tote and kept walking, focused on the small, immediate things: the weight of bread, the smell of herbs, the knowledge that Rowan would wake to flowers she hadn't chosen and soup she hadn't cooked—and that, for now, was enough.

He hoped.

Chapter Twenty-One

Rowan

When Ethan arrived back at the townhouse, Rowan watched him settle the girls in. Shoes were kicked off at the door. Grocery bags rustled in the kitchen. Down the hall came the sounds of negotiation from the back bedroom, punctuated by laughter and the unmistakable thump of a pillow hitting a wall.

Rowan sat, propped on the couch with a blanket over her knees, letting the movement ebb out of her. Fig occupied the armrest beside her like a small, offended gargoyle, green eyes narrowed as if the entire afternoon had been a personal inconvenience. The cat's tail flicked once, sharp and judgmental, registering what could only be an official complaint.

She closed her eyes and breathed through the ache under her ribs before lifting her chin toward the kitchen. It still smelled faintly of the citrus cleaner Ethan had used that morning. The house was clean, but she felt dirty.

Ethan wiped the counter, sweeping away the last bright remnants of his flower-decorating project. He moved with the easy focus he'd fallen into all week, dusting off the orange flecks caught in the lines of his palms.

She gathered her courage.

"I need a shower," she called. "I can do it myself if you can set me up."

She hated how careful the sentence sounded—hated that she'd rehearsed it in her head first.

Ethan didn't hesitate. "I've got you."

And the way he said it—simple, certain, no trace of bitterness—made her ribs tighten. Not with pain. With something else. Something inconvenient but warm.

Rowan shifted forward carefully, letting Ethan read the movement before offering his hand. He always did that—waiting half a beat, giving her the choice. She hated how much it mattered. She took his hand anyway.

In the bathroom, steam fogged the mirror as Ethan adjusted the water—warm, not hot—and moved anything that looked remotely capable of sending her back to the hospital. He straightened the bathmat and moved the bathroom stool just so. He stayed angled toward the door, giving her room to keep one hand braced on the counter like a guardrail.

"Okay?" he asked. "Step in. Hold here."

Rowan followed his voice more than his instructions. It grounded her. The steadiness of it, the absence of urgency, eased her through the familiar routine. He talked her through the shower in low, even phrases—where to place her feet, when to pause, when to breathe—offering help only when she reached for it.

She was acutely aware of him. Of how close he was. Of how

long it had been since proximity had felt like this—charged and careful all at once. He never looked where he shouldn't, even when her nerves hummed knowing that he could. That restraint made her chest ache worse than if he had.

When she stepped out, damp and unsteady, the energy shifted.

Ethan was there immediately, wrapping a towel around her with his hands firmly on her shoulders, his gaze deliberately fixed somewhere above her hairline. He reached for a second towel and began drying her hair, fingers working the terry cloth slowly at her scalp, soaking up water without pulling her curls.

Rowan swallowed.

It shouldn't have undone them.

It did.

She could see it in the way his shoulders eased, in the way his breathing slowed to match hers, as if he hadn't realized how tightly wound he'd been until this moment demanded gentleness.

"Good?" he asked quietly.

"Better," Rowan said—and then, without thinking, she tipped her head into his hand. Just for a second. An unguarded instinct. Long enough for heat to spark, quick and dangerous.

She caught herself, straightened, and smirked. "You missed a spot."

"I'd better rectify that," he said dryly.

Her mouth curved despite herself.

He helped her into fresh, soft clothes and guided her back down the hall, hands steady at her waist when the world tilted. She hated that she needed this. She hated it more that she liked trusting him with it.

"Okay?" he asked again.

"Okay," she said, then huffed a laugh. "Don't get any ideas."

"Too late," he said. "I had a whole list."

He eased her back onto the couch, tucked the blanket with practiced care, and set her water within reach. "Feeling better is the priority."

The girls glanced up—two quick assessments. Rosie clocked the way he adjusted a pillow without being asked, the way he checked Rowan's face before stepping back. Tiffany's smile went small and pleased, like she'd spotted something she liked and filed it away for later.

Ethan's phone buzzed. Rowan saw the moment it tugged at him—the reflexive glance, the flicker of something old and sharp. He checked the screen, then slid the phone under a magazine.

Not now.

For one dizzying second, she saw what he was seeing without him having to say it: a quiet weekend without a hospital wristband in the trash. The girls' laughter drifted down the hall. Burned pancakes. Mismatched flowers in a jar. The vision steadied her—and scared her.

It asked questions she knew neither of them was ready to answer.

"Dad?" Tiffany said.

"Yeah?"

She tilted her head, and her glue-smudged fingers paused mid-air. "It'd be nice if we had a mom and a dad. Like...here always."

The words landed softly. Not a demand. Not a plan. Just a truth offered the way kids offered wishes—with the confidence that wanting something didn't make it wrong.

Rowan froze, breath caught halfway in. She waited for Ethan to deflect. To joke. To redirect.

He didn't.

Rosie leaned closer to Tiffany, stage-whispering with all the subtlety of a seasoned director. "I think maybe we should give them a minute."

"A minute for what?" Tiffany asked.

Rosie shrugged. "Adult talking. Or tea refilling. Or...feeli ngs."

Rowan snorted despite herself. "We're right here."

"We know," Rosie said cheerfully. "We'll be over there."

They moved all of three feet away, whispering loudly and very much pretending not to watch.

Rowan smoothed a damp curl at her temple and caught Ethan's eyes over the rim of her mug. The warmth there wasn't accidental. It wasn't cautious either.

"Could you help with brushing my hair?" she murmured.

"Anytime," he said.

Tiffany squinted at their craft, then nodded decisively. "Okay. We're good."

Rosie lifted her marker and traced a large check in the air. "Done."

Ethan glanced between them. "What's done, exactly?"

"We'll tell you later." Rosie smiled, satisfied, then leaned toward her sister and whispered louder than intended, "We want to keep him."

Tiffany nodded, glue and glitter drying in silver constellations on her fingertips. "Obviously."

Rowan laughed—soft, real—and leaned back into the couch, surrounded by noise and warmth and the unmistakable sense that something fragile and important was taking shape.

Chapter Twenty-Two

Rowan

The townhouse was abnormally quiet.

Rain threaded softly against the window screen. From down the hall came the uneven hush of two girls who had fallen asleep mid-conversation—Tiffany had Shimmer Star tucked under her chin, Rosie dead to the world on the cot, one hand flung over her eyes like a melodramatic actress.

In the kitchen, Rowan stood at the sink with a plate she had no business washing. The lamp over the stove cast a warm circle on the counter, gilding the slope of her cheek. She tried to keep her ribs from pulling as she reached for the dish towel.

"Let me." Ethan's voice came from behind her, low, steady. He eased the plate from her hands and set it in the rack, then slid the towel out of reach.

She opened her mouth to argue on principle. The fight went out of her at the same time the ache tugged under her ribs.

"I'm moving," she said instead.

"Correct," he said, mouth curving.

She turned to shoo him and found herself closer than she had meant to be. The kitchen shrank to fit them. His sleeves were pushed up, and his forearms were damp from the sink. Her fingers were damp, too, from stubborn effort and cooling dishwater.

He tipped his head, eyes searching hers. "You okay?"

Rowan held his gaze and let the answer be simple. "Yes."

He reached, slow and sure, and cupped her jaw. His palm was warm; his thumb settled at the hinge. The steadiness of his touch stole the tightness from her shoulders. She rose onto her toes without thinking, one hand finding the flat of his chest, feeling the strong, quiet beat under cotton.

The first brush of his mouth was careful. The second had heat.

A slow slide of lips and air and something she recognized from their past, only steadier now. She answered with the smallest sound, fingers curling in his shirt to keep from leaning too hard, to keep from forgetting what her body could handle.

Her body answered anyway and then reminded her she'd been cut open. A tug, small but real, caught sharp under her ribs. She drew in a quick breath.

He felt it before she could step back. He broke the kiss, forehead resting against hers, breath rough. His thumb stroked once along her cheek, apology and promise in a single pass. "Not yet," he said, voice frayed with want and restraint.

She huffed a laugh that shook and held. The words shouldn't have made her flush, but they did. *Not yet was a promise, not an ending.*

"Ask me again when I'm not on day and night pain meds,"

she murmured.

"I plan to," he said. His other hand slid from her jaw to the nape of her neck, fingers finding the knot of the floral scarf she'd used to pull back her hair, holding there like he was steadying her and himself at once.

They stood like that for a long heartbeat, breathing the same square of air, and then he eased back, fingers slipping from her jaw. He skimmed his knuckles over the inside of her wrist—a lingering, reverent touch that sent a bright line of heat up her arm—then stepped aside.

"Couch?" he asked softly. "Old movie, low volume, no heroics, and only smart women."

"Approved," she said.

He waited while she set a palm on the counter and took the slow steps that made her feel steady. He braced a hand at the edge of the counter, close enough to catch, far enough to let her do the walking.

In the living room, the teal-and-gold banner lifted when the heater clicked on. Fig relocated to the back of the couch with a short mew. Ethan found the remote and flipped until grainy black-and-white images filled the screen. A couple on a rain-soaked street argued like it was foreplay, then laughed like no one was watching.

Rowan settled into the couch. He took the space beside her, close enough that their knees touched. Warmth seeped through the thin knit of her lounge pants where his leg pressed into hers. He offered his hand.

She laced their fingers and let the quiet do most of the talking.

"Thank you...for everything," she said, eyes on the screen, voice low so it wouldn't travel to the girls' room.

"You don't have to keep thanking me," he said, thumb tracing her knuckles, a slow arc he returned to without thinking. "I like being here."

She angled toward him, careful, and let her head tip to his shoulder. He went still for half a second, then relaxed into the shape of them. He turned his face enough that his breath moved along her temple. The movie murmured while the rain kept time on the window. Their joined hands rested warm on her thigh. He shifted once, not to pull away, but to tuck her closer, one broad hand settling on the outside of her thigh, heat sinking through cotton to skin.

"You were brave tonight," he said after a while, still watching the screen.

"For letting you wash a plate?" She smiled into his shirt.

"For letting me in," he said. "For saying things it hurts to say."

She breathed him in—soap, clean cotton, the faint cedar that clung to him now—ordinary things that had started to feel like home. "You stopped when I needed you to stop."

"Always," he said. His mouth brushed her hairline, a near-kiss that still counted.

She twined their fingers tighter. "If I say yes to this," she said, the words quiet and steady, "I need patience. I need the boring days. I need you to tell me the hard things before they bang on the door."

His hand tightened, not just a squeeze, but a vow. "You get my yes on the slow days. I'll be honest, even when my pride wants to be loud. And when you need space, I will give it without leaving you alone in the room."

She let that settle. "And you?"

"I need you to tell me when I'm trying too hard, before I start fixing things that aren't broken." He tipped his head until his cheek rested against hers. "And I need you to believe me when I say I'm in."

She didn't say she believed him. She showed it, sliding their joined hands higher on her thigh until his thumb spread in a wide, warm line at the hem of her shorts. The little claim loosened something in his breath.

They watched the couple onscreen get it wrong, then get it right, then get it wrong again. Fig turned once and collapsed in a puddle of cat in the hollow behind Rowan's knees.

"Ethan?"

"Yeah."

Her voice softened until it was barely more than a whisper. "Kiss me again. Slow."

Chapter Twenty-Three

Ethan

Ethan's phone started vibrating before dawn, a hard little buzz against the coffee table that felt louder than it should. He landed a palm on it, saw the Manhattan timestamp, and stepped onto the front porch so he wouldn't wake anyone.

Harrison didn't bother with hello. "We need you here in person for Thursday's distributor pitch. The buyers are coming in hot. It's a room-read situation."

Ethan leaned against the porch rail, the cool air clearing the last of sleep from his head. The street was still. Somewhere, a sprinkler ticked on. Behind him, the house hummed—heat, pipes, the small sounds of people sleeping.

Thursday.

A Manhattan Thursday came easily: the long table, the glass walls, the practiced rhythm of a pitch he could run on instinct.

Then another Thursday rose just as quickly: Tiffany's tide pool field trip. The permission slip on the fridge. Her careful warning about waves, rocks, and losing your shoes.

He could do both. But he couldn't be in both places.

Ethan looked back through the dark window at the quiet townhouse; at the shape of a life he was expanding to fill.

The answer didn't arrive like a revelation.

It came as a relief.

"I can't fly this week," he said. "I'll lead the deck remotely. You'll have my numbers and my talking points. Brad can handle the handshakes."

A beat of professional silence. "Remote is not our preference."

"I know." He pressed two fingers to the bridge of his nose and pictured Rowan asleep down the hall, her flowered scarf looped on the chair by her bed. "But it's what I can give. I'll send the revised margin sheets at nine your time and hold prep calls, then I'm on for the pitch. I need to be done by nine a.m. Pacific. We won't lose them because I'm not in the chair."

On the other end, he listened to the indistinct murmur of a conference room—doors, paper, the scrape of chairs. "We'll take it," Harrison said at last. "But this can't keep happening, Ethan."

He'd earned the warning. He kept his voice even. "I'm aware."

When the call ended, he sagged against the railing for a second and let the quiet settle.

By the time he rounded the corner into the kitchen, it had softened into morning. Rosie stood at the counter with a cutting board, slicing a cucumber into tidy half-moons and laying them carefully across a paper towel.

"Presentation matters," she said without looking up. "Also,

soggy cucumbers are gross."

"Strong language before coffee," he said.

She grinned. "Mom says the same thing."

Tiffany sat at the table with a pencil and a stack of worksheets, erasing with gentle rubs and fixing a line of math. She glanced at him, then at the hallway, then back to her work, as if making sure all the pieces were where they should be.

Rowan padded in a few minutes later, bundled in a fuzzy yellow robe. The color made her cheeks look warmer than they had a few days before. She took in the table, the knife in Rosie's hand, the sandwich fixings, the way Tiffany had lined up her folders by size.

"Morning," she said, voice low from sleep. "Tea first."

"Herbal, honey, on the way," Ethan said, already reaching for the kettle.

Rowan's gaze slid to the phone on the counter, then to his face. She didn't ask. He liked her more for it.

"Let's add grapes to lunch," Rosie announced, tugging open the fridge. "Not just cucumbers. Variety is important."

"Variety is also complicated," Ethan said, but he made room on the counter. Tiffany leaned over to inspect his knife work and nodded solemnly when he cut the crusts into neat corners.

Rowan watched him move through the kitchen with an expression that made his chest ache in a way he didn't mind.

"Okay, Tiffany, you got the lunch, but don't forget it's Monday. Please grab your library book."

"But I'm not—" She looked at Ethan, then Rowan, before closing her mouth. "Okay."

They walked towards the door together when it was time to

find shoes and jackets. Rosie didn't wait to be asked. She zipped Tiffany's coat and tucked a stray wisp of hair into the collar with gentle efficiency. At the door, Tiffany checked her backpack twice, then a third time for good measure. She hesitated and looked up.

"You'll be there at two-thirty?"

"Two-thirty," he said. "Early."

At the car, Ethan's phone buzzed with a reminder for the morning prep call. He silenced it and opened the passenger door for Rosie.

"You're going to be late for your important empire thing," she said as she swung in.

He looked at her. Smart. Bossy. Nine going on forty. "I scheduled around you."

Her mouth curved. "Obviously."

Back at the townhouse, he set his laptop on the coffee table, made one last pass through the deck, and sent Harrison the revised margin model with a clean subject line.

When his prep call started, Ethan took the corner of the couch where he could see the hallway. He walked them through the numbers like he'd promised—freight offsets, glass savings on the sampler, a clean hook for the endcaps. Brad pushed a little too hard on the closing numbers, and Ethan nudged him toward a line that would land better with the buyer.

It was muscle memory.

It just felt different with Rowan's tea mug two inches from

his trackpad and a pink octopus staring solemnly from the arm of the couch.

He ended the call and closed the laptop when Fig expressed her opinion that a snack was overdue. The space softened back into real life.

Rowan stood by the window with her tea, sunlight catching the large gold hoops in her ears. She tilted her head toward him. "They wanted you there."

"They did."

"But you didn't go." She didn't dress it up, and neither did he. There was more to it than the words.

"I'll make time to catch up next week," he said. "When you're feeling better."

Rowan watched him, then let out a small breath. She didn't release the flood of things he could see waiting behind her eyes. She gave him a tight smile and a nod.

The rest of the morning was spent on small tasks. He reset the medication alarms. He wrote *'science project' on the calendar because Tiffany had mentioned it three times in the last two days,* with a mix of pride and dread.

When he picked her up after school, her shoulders were high and tight in the way they got when she was worried about too many things.

"I think we need to be productive." He announced as she climbed in. "We're making a project supply run. We will not be the family who does the volcano last minute at eleven at night."

"We don't do volcanoes," she said, outraged. "We're sprouting beans in jars. It's biology. Mom says life starts small and quiet."

He swallowed against the truth of that and grinned. "Beans it is."

They stopped for mason jars and cotton balls. Tiffany debated between pinto and lima beans, then chose both on the grounds of "varied data."

Back at the townhouse, Rosie helped her rinse the beans—because she lived on a farm and knew about gardening—and they set up a line of jars on the windowsill where the afternoon light pooled.

Tiffany set up a growth chart and drew labels in block letters, while Rosie added tiny crowns to the plant tags for reasons no one could explain.

After dinner, when the table held only crumbs, the girls were arguing over who got the good pen for drawing or charting. Tiffany turned with sudden seriousness and addressed Rowan.

"Dad said no to a big fancy work thing because he promised to help me with my science project after school," she said matter-of-factly. "He stayed."

Rowan blinked once, hard, then let the relief show. She looked at Ethan, and that was worse and better than anything she could have said.

"I'm glad," she said. "I like beans better than boardrooms."

"Unpopular opinion," he said, and the small smile she gave him would carry him farther than he'd admit.

He caught Tiffany watching him, something close to awe bright and unguarded in her face. He realized, as cleanly as if someone had told him, that she was filing this away. *This is what it looks like when Dad says something and then does it.* His throat tightened in a way work had never done to him.

He cleared it gently. "Tonight's Rosie's last night."

"Boo," Tiffany said, trying to sound brave, but the small tear at the corner of her eye said otherwise.

"There are still four chapters left in the bear book!" Rosie protested.

"I think," Ethan said, rubbing his chin, "we need a bear-book marathon. We'll get ready for bed early and read until we hit the last page—or both of you are asleep."

"Deal!" they yelled together.

Chapter Twenty-Four

Ethan

The next day slipped by too quickly.

Rosie walked Tiffany into school one last time, backpack bouncing, offering unsolicited advice about lockers and snack trades, as if she were leaving a field manual behind.

They detoured for bubble tea afterward. Rosie insisted Rowan try some, watching with fierce concentration until she took a careful sip and admitted it was "surprisingly good."

By the time they circled back to the school that afternoon, the hours already felt spent. Rosie and Tiffany tangled together in the pickup line, all elbows and whispered promises, and the car filled with the strange, buzzy quiet that comes when everyone is preparing for what comes next.

Ethan eased the car into Park, and the three of them spilled into the noise—rollers thumping over tile, a loudspeaker insisting someone return to security, the smell of fries drifting from a kiosk. Rosie clutched her backpack, excitement and dread wrestling on her face. Tiffany kept one hand on Ethan's sleeve like an anchor, her lips pressed flat.

"Gate B," Ethan said, reading the board. "We've got time."

They moved as a unit through check-in and toward the security line, where an attendant waved them into the "authorized escort" lane. Rosie squeezed Tiffany's fingers twice.

"Text me when you land," Tiffany said, voice small but sure.

"I'll send a picture of the clouds," Rosie promised, then glanced up at Ethan. "And I'll text Dad when I'm back with Mom."

"Good," he said, swallowing around the tight band in his throat. "I love to see your face, kiddo."

Past security, the gate area buzzed. Families spread picnic-style across the carpet. A toddler in dinosaur pajamas did laps around a column while his mother chased after him with a shoe. Rosie tugged open her backpack and rifled through the front pocket with purpose.

"Hold out your wrist," she told Tiffany.

Tiffany blinked. "Why?"

"You can't say goodbye without something," Rosie said, as if that were in every rule book worth reading. She dug into her backpack and pulled out two thin bracelets—teal and gold, elastic threaded with small, faceted beads. "Sisters forever."

Tiffany's breath hitched. "One for each of us..."

They tied the bracelets onto one another's wrists with careful fingers, then held them out to compare.

"Just a little longer," Ethan said gently. "Let's grab a seat over there."

They sat side by side on a row of vacant chairs, legs not touching, their new matching bracelets glinting under the gate's fluorescent lights.

A gate agent called families with small children. Rosie's boarding group would be next.

Tiffany stared at the carpet. "I hate this part."

"I know," Rosie said, then touched her shoulder. "Thursday is your field trip. Send me pictures. And don't let Dad fall on a slippery rock."

"I wish you were there to boss him." Tiffany's mouth wobbled. "You're better at it."

Rosie tried for a grin and got halfway there. "Obviously."

When the boarding call came, it came fast. Rosie turned to Ethan and stepped into his chest with more force than she meant to.

He folded her in and breathed in the cotton and sugar that was pure Rosie. "You are so brave," he said into her hair. "I'm proud of you."

She tipped her head back. "Don't let Tiffany feel alone."

"We won't," he said.

He crouched to Tiffany's level. "You okay?"

Tiffany nodded, then shook her head, then nodded again. "I don't like the part where people leave."

He didn't tell her it was fine. He didn't tell her to be tough. He held out his arms. She stepped in, small body rigid at first, then melting the way she did when she decided a person had earned it.

"It hurts because it matters," he said into the top of her head. "That's a good sign."

Rosie looped her arms around both of them, a tangle of elbows, backpacks, and bracelets.

When the gate agent called for final boarding, Rosie wiped her face with the heel of her palm and squared her shoulders like a tiny soldier.

"I'm going," she said. "I love you guys."

"Love you," Tiffany said quickly, the words spilling out in a rush before she could swallow them.

Ethan stood and dropped a kiss on Rosie's forehead. "Text me when you're buckled."

She walked toward the jetway, then turned and ran back three steps to whisper something into Tiffany's ear that made Tiffany's face crumple and then smooth. Rosie pressed her palm to the teal-and-gold beads and went.

They watched until the last flash of wild hair disappeared down the ramp.

Chapter Twenty-Five

Rowan

Back at the townhouse, Rowan had propped herself against the couch pillows, wearing vibrant, geometric-patterned pajamas.

When they walked through the door, she reached toward Tiffany. "Hey, baby."

Tiffany crossed the room fast and folded herself in—careful of the incision, careful of everything. Rowan held as much of her as she could, and even that pull cost her. She hid the wince and pressed her nose to her daughter's hair.

"She got on the plane?" Rowan asked, eyes on Ethan.

He nodded. "Brave face."

Tiffany sat back, cheeks blotchy, and tugged her sleeve up to show the bracelet. "We matched." Her mouth trembled. "She's not here."

"No," Rowan said, the word blunt and true. "She's not."

Ethan hovered with too much energy for the quiet in the room. "We could make popcorn and watch a movie," he said, already reaching for the cabinet. "Or start those bean observations."

Rowan's eyes flicked to him. "Give her a minute."

"I'm trying to help," he said, the defensive edge surprising both of them.

"I know," Rowan said, gentle and steady. "Let it be sad for a second."

Tiffany heard them. Her shoulders rose and dropped, and then the tears came, hot and silent, a leak she'd been holding back since the gate. Rowan opened her arms. Tiffany climbed in, and Rowan's hand found circles along her back, slow and even.

Ethan stood there with a bag of corn kernels in his hand, helpless in the face of sorrow he couldn't fix. He set the bag down and crossed the room. He didn't hover. He didn't leave.

After the storm passed, Tiffany hiccupped once and swiped at her face with her sleeve. "I'm okay."

"You are," Rowan said. "You don't have to make a show of it."

"Would popcorn be allowed now?" Tiffany asked, trying to be practical.

"Popcorn is always allowed," Ethan said, grateful for orders he could follow.

He moved to the kitchen, put the pot on the stove, and listened to the first kernels hit the hot oil. Behind him, he heard Rowan's breath catch on a small pull she couldn't hide. He turned in time to see her ease back into the pillows, eyes pinched for a second.

"You should lie down in your room," he said before he softened it. "That sounded rough."

Her chin tipped, stubborn. "I'm fine."

He looked at the set of her mouth and then at the girl tucked into her side. He didn't press. He drained the popcorn into a bowl and dusted it with a happy amount of salt, the sound of kernels hitting ceramic filling the space the way he'd hoped his words wouldn't.

They ate on the couch, feet tucked, Fig pretending not to beg and failing. Tiffany leaned against Rowan with the weight of a girl who had earned herself the right to be tired. When the bowl was half gone, Ethan slid his hand to the arm of the couch and set his palm up. Tiffany's fingers found it, a small, sure fit.

He put on a nature documentary, the kind with calm narration and ocean sounds. Tiffany watched the jellies, eyes steady, lashes wet. Rowan's breath evened out. He saw the moment the pain caught up, and the energy ran out. She didn't say it. She never did.

"Let's get you two in bed early," he said quietly. "We can find a new bedtime book."

Tiffany nodded and went to brush her teeth without argument, a sure sign she was past the worst of it. When she was done, she came back to the couch and wrapped both arms around Rowan again, careful, always careful. "Goodnight, Mom."

"Goodnight," Rowan said, voice gone husky. "I love you to the moon and back."

"I know." Tiffany hesitated, then added, "Me too."

Ethan tucked Tiffany in and waited until her breathing smoothed before he returned to the living room. Rowan hadn't moved much, but her shoulders sat lower now, and the lines around her mouth had softened.

"I'm not trying to override you," he said, standing on the other side of the coffee table, words pitched low so they wouldn't carry down the hall. "I just hate that she hurts."

"I know," Rowan said. "I hate it too."

He sank into the chair across from her, elbows on his knees. "Sometimes my brain goes straight to distractions and plans, and new goals like that will fix things."

"Sometimes it helps," she admitted. "Sometimes it makes everything louder." Rowan smiled and fidgeted with her earrings. "Do you remember the night Tiffany was born?"

His eyes lifted fast, then softened. "I think about it more than I let myself admit."

"Me too." The memory hit hard and clean: tile and fluorescent light and fear she had made into a habit. "I was scared. I didn't want to be, but I was. I had this picture in my head of the kind of mother I wanted to be."

He didn't jump in. He waited, steady.

"I called you," she said, her voice thinner. "You said you were coming. Then the meeting moved. Remember?"

He looked wrecked in a way that didn't ask her to comfort him.

"I remember every ugly detail, and I wish I could rewrite that night. My flight got pushed. I told myself I'd still make it. Then I told myself you'd be better off without the chaos of a last-minute arrival. I told myself a lot of things. None of them were the right thing."

"I told myself I could do it alone," she said, because she had, and because that lie had been comfortable enough to keep for years. "And I did. But not because it was noble. Because I was afraid to need you and then have you go anyway."

He stared at his hands, then turned one palm up on the cushion between them, an offering. "I should have shown up even if you didn't answer my call," he said, voice low and sure. "I should have taken the next flight, stood in the lobby, and demanded the nurse let me carry your bag. I let work be the reason because it was neat. Life isn't neat. That's on me."

Something under her ribs loosened. It wasn't forgiveness so much as oxygen. "We were both stubborn," she said. "You hid in success. I hid in strength. We built walls and called them plans."

"I don't want to be that man," he said, meeting her gaze. "I like the one I'm becoming."

She pictured him in that clumsy green-and-white party room, knife in hand and pride held together with a joke, and something warm grabbed hold of her ribs right where the stitches tugged. "I like him too."

Chapter Twenty-Six

Ethan

By the time Ethan climbed the steps of the field trip school bus, he'd already lived two days.

The first belonged to Manhattan.

A screen full of faces at a long table, he wasn't sitting at. He'd walked the pitch deck as East Coast sunshine poured through skyscraper windows, and Rowan's townhouse remained in darkness. They covered freight margins and shelf placement. He could see their curiosity, even if he couldn't be there with them. He thought it went well, but he wouldn't know for sure until contracts started moving and optimism turned into ink.

The second belonged to the quiet aftermath. A West Coast dawn. One lone backpack on a hook. Rowan was moving slowly, but moving—insisting on making toast, taking her own meds, and not being watched so closely. Tiffany checked the clock twice and pretended not to as they headed for school.

By the time the bus pulled out of the school parking lot, he was running on anxiety and a resilient tiredness no amount of caffeine could beat. He rolled his shoulders once, put his phone on silent, and told himself the only numbers that mattered for the next few hours were tide charts and head counts.

Saltwater State Park smelled of seaweed and wood smoke. Gulls wheeled over the gray-green water while a ranger in a windbreaker pointed with a laminated map and talked about the magic word of the day: low tide.

"Rules," Ms. Barlow called, lifting her clipboard. "Two-finger touch. No prying, no flipping large rocks, watch the waves. If your shoes get soaked, that's on you." She added, with a look that made twenty-eight third graders freeze, "And nobody climbs the big outcropping. It's slippery."

Ethan stood with his four assigned kids. Tiffany, in her heart-pocket raincoat, listened politely. Caleb, the gap-toothed boy from the craft club, was already bouncing on his toes. Noor adjusted her knit hat and held her scavenger hunt sheet like a life vest. Logan hummed the theme music to an imaginary movie and tried to see how far he could jump from one wet rock to another without dying.

Ethan did a quick headcount while the ranger passed out pencils. His phone buzzed with a Manhattan number he didn't need to look at. He let it buzz.

Ms. Barlow clapped. "Scavenger buddies, go!"

The beach unfolded in a series of small pools that held tiny worlds—green anemones that closed when a child's fingers touched them, limpets clamped to rocks, sea stars tucked under ledges, waving their small arms. The sky was the color of oyster shells. Cold seeped through their shoes, even when the sand looked dry.

"These anemones look like flowers," Noor said, kneeling beside Tiffany. "But with teeth."

"They're sticky," Tiffany said. "They don't hurt."

"Two-finger touch," Ethan reminded, then eased Logan one step back from a slick shelf. "We keep our feet on sand or low rocks. The big ones are off-limits."

Caleb held up a crab molt like a treasure. "I found armor."

"On the list," Ethan said, and checked a box. The tide made a soft shushing sound along the beach. He felt the pull of the horizon and a smaller tug under his ribs that had Rowan's name on it. She'd been pale over tea this morning, determined to do too much. He'd wanted to fuss, and she had lifted her chin. They'd met in the middle, or so he hoped.

"Mr. Moore!" Logan waved from a tide pool the size of a kiddie pool. "Is this a mussel or a rock pretending?"

"Mussel," Ethan said, crouching. "See lines of the shell?"

Logan lit up and tried counting the lines one by one. Noor found a tiny hermit crab and whispered to it to avoid scaring it. Caleb squinted at barnacles and declared them "mini volcanoes."

Ethan turned to ask Tiffany about her list.

She wasn't next to him.

"Tiff?" He pivoted. She'd been here, close enough to touch, one hand on his sleeve, a minute ago.

"Over here!" Noor called.

False alarm, because she meant the hermit crab and not Tiffany.

A shout rolled down the shore. "Hey! Off the rocks!"

He saw her then, a tiny figure in her pink coat halfway up the slick outcropping the ranger had pointed to, trying to reach a round, sun-glossed pool tucked into a notch where the water had left a necklace of shells. A glint of gold caught sunlight—Tiffany's bracelet flashed when she stretched.

"Dad, the scavenger list says chiton," she called back, careful and proud. "They like the high rocks."

Another shout came from farther down. "Careful!"

"Stop there." Ethan's voice came out too calm for what ran through him. "Tiff, freeze. I'm coming."

He looked at his group. "Noor, can you grab Ms. Barlow? Caleb, Logan, you stay with her." He pointed to another chaperone—a dad in a Seahawks cap. "Can you keep an eye on my three?"

"Got them," the man said.

Ethan picked his way across the wet rocks, choosing each step carefully. The world narrowed to the slick sheen of algae under his boots. Tiffany turned to grin at him and then vanished with a cry.

"Tiffany!" He yelled, trying to move faster towards where she'd been.

The rock ledge dropped into a narrow crack, the kind the sea had been chewing for a century. Water surged at the bottom. Tiffany wedged in the cleft shoulder-deep, one leg dangling. Her hands were up, palms flat against the stone.

"I'm okay," she said, too quickly. The water lapped and hissed around her sneakers.

Ethan dropped to his knees and reached into the cold. Barnacles bit his skin. He found her forearm and wrapped his hand around it carefully. "You're safe. I've got you."

Her face tipped toward him, pale and determined. "My ankle got stuck. I slipped."

"Can you move your toes?"

She wiggled them, then winced. "Kind of."

"Good." He looked at the way she'd fallen. If he yanked, she'd scrape herself raw. The next wave sloshed an inch higher up the crack. He wedged his boots against the rock and breathed past the tightness clawing up his throat.

"Talk to me," she said, small but steady. "Mom says when I get scared, it's okay to say it out loud."

He laughed without meaning to, a quick sound that let him breathe. "Your mom is smarter than me."

"I know," she said. "But you're strong. Strong is also helpful."

"Strong is useful right now." He braced, shifted his grip to get under her arm, and slid his other hand down until he could cup behind her knee. The water surged again, cold and mean. He tried to move, and his bruised knuckles scraped the rock. The world narrowed further: a green smear, her wrist tiny in his hand, the hiss that made his lungs forget how to pull air.

"Okay," Tiffany whispered, as if she'd felt the spin. "In three counts. Out, four." Her own breath came steadily. "You taught me that when you were putting out the broccoli fire."

"In," he said, and obeyed his eight-year-old. "Three. Out. Four."

The throbbing in his ears eased enough that he could think. He waited for the water to ebb, then lifted when the crack ran drier. She tried to help, face screwed up with effort, and then her knee cleared, and she popped free like a cork, sliding forward into his chest. He staggered back two steps, then sat down hard in the wet because his legs didn't trust him yet.

Tiffany clung for a heartbeat, then pushed her hair out of her eyes. "Ow."

"Ankle?"

She nodded, lip caught between her teeth.

Ms. Barlow's boots thudded behind him. "You two okay?"

"Took a tumble," Ethan said, voice rough. "We need ice and a bench."

Ms. Barlow knelt, eyes scanning Tiffany quickly and competently. "No blood. Good color. Let's not test it. We'll piggyback."

"I can walk," Tiffany said, defiant even now.

Just like her mother, Ethan thought.

"Not on a sprain," Ms. Barlow said. She looked up at him. "You good?"

"I am," he said, and meant the parts that mattered.

He crouched and tucked Tiffany up onto his back, feeling the small, familiar weight of her settle against his shoulders. She wrapped her arms loosely around his neck—not choking, just holding. He stood up carefully, one foot then the other, and followed Ms. Barlow toward the picnic tables at the edge of the grass.

Kids streamed past with treasures: a feather, a perfect shell, the dramatic retelling of a crab that had chased a boy like a tiny soldier.

"You scared me," he said into the wind, fierce and soft all at once.

"I scared me too," Tiffany admitted.

"What happened? You knew not to go on those rocks."

"I know, but Rosie would have done it." She shifted slightly, then added, as if this mattered too, "The chiton was extremely cool."

His chest tightened. Of course, it had been. She'd been braver lately. Louder. Testing herself in small ways—new foods, new opinions, extra space in the world.

"I'm glad you're trying new things," he said, giving a little bounce to move her back towards his shoulders. "I know you're strong like your mom, and brave like your sister. But you're also you."

She was quiet.

"You are very smart—"

"And going on the rocks wasn't smart," she finished.

He breathed once before answering. "No. It wasn't. Maybe someday, with help. But today, you were asked to avoid that area, and you knew it."

"Yeah," she said. "I thought it was just a little way."

"Pushing boundaries can be good," he said—*like telling your employer your family mattered more.* "But next time, I need you to use this." He smiled and tapped his forehead.

He hugged her as carefully as he could with her on his back. When he looked up, Ms. Barlow was waiting, listening. She nodded once, approving, then crossed to a nearby table where another parent produced a first-aid kit like he'd been ready for this exact moment.

Ethan lowered her onto the edge of the table, and Ms. Barlow wrapped Tiffany's ankle in an ace bandage and handed

Ethan a gallon zip bag full of ice. He settled it over the wrap and held it there while Tiffany hissed, then slowly relaxed into the cold.

"We're going to skip the rest of the tide pool time for you today," Ms. Barlow said gently. "You get a job with me. Clipboard manager."

Tiffany nodded solemnly. "I like clipboards."

"I know," Ms. Barlow said.

Ethan sat back, hands wet and stinging. He turned them over and saw small cuts along his knuckles where barnacles had kissed skin. The sting barely registered compared to the way his ribs tried—and failed—to settle.

Tiffany was safe.

She was breathing.

She was right there.

His hands were shaking.

What he felt was an echo.

Fear was still moving through him. Relief arriving late. The certainty, sudden and unarguable, that there was no meeting on earth worth trading this for. He let himself feel it—the fear, the relief, the unsteady gratitude of being exactly where he was supposed to be when it mattered.

Not in a boardroom.

Not on a screen.

Here.

Chapter Twenty-Seven

Ethan

The Ladder H demands were growing harder to keep up with.

He'd delayed them until he got home from the field trip, but the second he could call New York, they had him tied up in last-minute contract negotiations. The buyers liked the distribution pitch, as he'd suspected, but they wanted firmer assurances on margins.

Ethan had the deck up, the camera off, and his laptop on the coffee table.

"Run the margin slide one more time," Harrison said. "They'll push on freight."

"I've got it," Ethan said. "Sampler glass cuts weight. We make it back on movement."

Next to him at the table, Tiffany sat with her foot elevated on a stool, tongue caught between her teeth as she painted a bear on a card for Rosie. A small cup of water to rinse her brush sat near her elbow. At the counter, Rowan checked the water in the bean cups.

"Ethan?" someone from the distributor cut in. "Speak to week-three endcaps?"

"Placement is—" He reached to unmute and caught Tiffany sliding the card closer so he could see. "Nice," he mouthed. Her face lit.

His finger hit the trackpad as the rinse cup tipped.

Paint water slicked across the keyboard.

"No," he barked.

Tiffany jolted. She grabbed for the cup, her little hand shaking, and sent another wash across the space bar.

"Leave it," he snapped. "Just—stop."

She froze.

Then she bolted down the hall.

Silence pulled tight.

Harrison said something about back panels. Ethan killed the mic and closed the laptop. Paint water clung to his hands.

"She's eight," Rowan said, cool and clear. "Not your intern."

He looked up, stung. "She's eight near my work. I asked for ten minutes."

"You asked for five, and you've been taking up space to work here all week," Rowan said, pushing off the counter. Color had returned to her cheeks, but fatigue edged it. "You keep planting your laptop in the middle of our lives and calling it a compromise."

He stood. "I'm trying to do both. I'm trying to make this work."

"You're trying to run it," she said. "My kitchen. My schedule. My kid."

Ethan stopped because this wasn't really about a laptop. Or a spill.

"You asked me to be here, then take the wheel back when it's hard. You want me close, but not close enough to be inconvenient." He took a breath. "Rowan, I'm still learning too."

"I've done this alone," she said. "Now you're here, rearranging drawers and explaining the better way to load the dishwasher. It feels like a takeover, not help."

A small breath hitched down the hall.

Then quiet sobs.

Ethan swallowed. "We can talk," he said, voice stripped down. "I'll fix the laptop later. I'm going to her."

Rowan stepped aside.

He knocked, then eased Tiffany's door open. She sat on the bed, knees up, the octopus pressed to her chest. Tears streaked her cheeks. Her chin tucked in that stubborn way she used when she refused to fall apart.

He knelt at her eye level. "Hey. That was on me. I shouldn't have snapped."

"I ruined your work."

"You didn't break anything that matters." He rested his glittered hands on his knees. "The laptop will survive. If it doesn't, I'll buy another. You're not replaceable."

She studied his face. "You yelled."

"I did. I was stressed and took it out on you. That was wrong."

"I didn't mean—"

"I know. I saw your drawing and wanted to tell you it was perfect, and then I chose a computer instead."

She blinked. "You and Mom are fighting."

The truth landed hard.

He held out his hand. "I'm going to try to fix what I can today. Okay?"

She slid her smaller hand into his. He felt the tremor and kept his grip gentle.

"We'll clean the keyboard keys. We'll move art away from the splash zone. And from now on, I won't bring a computer into common spaces. If I need to call New York, I'll do it in the bedroom."

"Are you mad at Mom?"

"I'm mad at myself. Your mom and I said things that didn't come out right. We'll untangle them."

"I guess you still have more to learn," she said, almost wryly.

"Absolutely, and I hope you keep helping me." He brushed a curl from her forehead. "Even if that's just being patient and waiting while I figure out how to make this work."

"That's what I want."

"Me too." He shifted. "Can I carry you to the couch? Sushi owes you a movie."

She smiled, small and real. "Sushi."

He lifted her, minding the wrap at her ankle, and carried her back.

Rowan had a towel and a small hairdryer in hand. She checked Tiffany first.

"You okay?"

Tiffany nodded. "We're good."

Rowan looked at Ethan. The air still held a storm's leftover charge.

"I'm sorry," he said before pride could catch up. "Wrong thing. Wrong tone."Her shoulders loosened. "I'm sorry too. I keep waiting for you to leave, so I kick first."He let it land. "I'm not leaving. But we do need to figure out how to do this together."

They didn't kiss it better.

They sat on the floor, side by side, tiny screws in a dish, a towel spread between them. He worked carefully at the laptop's seams, blotting moisture from its cracks and crevices. Faint streaks of paint dried across his knuckles.

Tiffany watched a cartoon at low volume and ate apple slices in neat bites, her eyes flicking to them until she settled.

The townhouse exhaled.

In the soft, shifting light of the television, Rowan rested a hand on the couch. "I really am sorry."

He sat with his elbows on his knees, the laptop closed and drying on the towel. A photo from the spaghetti place glowed on his phone—two girls with smiles as wide as their eyes. "Me, too."

"I don't want you to fix us," she said, stepping closer. "I want you to stay with us."

He looked up, clear and wrecked at once. "Then I need to figure out how. Not a plan. A life."

She sat. Their shoulders touched. He slid his hand across the cushion until his fingers found hers. She laced them.

Rain tapped the kitchen window. On the sill, a lima bean had split a little more, a thin white root easing into a new world.

"We'll keep growing," she said.

"Absolutely," he said, and meant it.

Everyone was tired. The day—built of responsibility and excitement—had been both rewarding and hard.

By the time Tiffany was in her pajamas, the house had gone quiet: dishes done, lights dimmed, Rowan's low voice drifting once down the hall for a second good night before a door closed.

Ethan carried Tiffany into her room, the ace wrap bright against the soft cotton of her leggings. He eased her onto the bed and arranged the pillows the way she liked: one at her back, one under her bad ankle. She watched him as he slipped the ice pack into its towel and laid it gently across her shin.

"Too cold?"

"It's okay."

"It should be a lot better tomorrow."

She nodded, then hesitated. "You were scared today."

Not a question.

"I was."

She picked at the blanket. "I talked to you like Mom talks to me."

He smiled. "It worked."

"I like your kind of brave."

"I like yours."

The lamp threw a warm oval across the wall, catching the glow-in-the-dark stars she'd never taken down.

"I like that you came," she said, almost too quiet to hear.

He sat back on his heels and looked at her—safe, pink-cheeked, eyelids heavy. "I'm always going to come," he said. Not big. Not loud. Just true.

She nodded once.

After a short bedtime book and the dark, she stopped him with a small hand around his wrist.

"Are you in trouble?"

"With who?"

"Mom."

He smiled into the dim. "Your mom's still upset about the rock. And she's going to be annoyed a little longer. But we'll talk, and we'll get better together."

"She will tell you she can lift the heavy things by herself," Tiffany said sleepily.

"She will."

He tucked the blanket under her chin and glanced at the teal-and-gold bracelet on her wrist—the perfect match to the one her sister wore so far away.

He brushed a kiss on her hair.

"Goodnight, kiddo."

"Night, Dad."

As he stood, she was already drifting, one hand curled around the bracelet, the other open on the quilt.

In the hallway, the house breathed.

And for the first time since the rocks, since the slip, since the sound of her cry cutting the wind, Ethan let himself breathe too.

The day was finally over.

Chapter Twenty-Eight

Rowan

Rowan lay awake, watching the ceiling lighten. Sleep had been stubborn. Every time she closed her eyes, she saw a pink raincoat halfway up a forbidden rock, a flash of teal-and-gold at a small wrist, Ethan's hands reaching into cold water.

The ice packed in the freezer thumped when the ice maker dumped a fresh tray. The sound snapped her back into the room. Fig, curled up at the foot of the bed, blinked at her curiously.

She felt almost normal. The ache in her incision was still there, but it didn't claw anymore. That urge she'd relied on for years kicked in: get up, do the list, put the world back where it belonged before anyone got ideas about handling it for you.

In the kitchen, someone wrestled with the toaster. The cat yowled a long complaint as she shifted in the bed, slid her feet to the floor, and promptly forgot she was supposed to be resting.

When she made it down the hall, she found Tiffany in the kitchen propped at the table with her foot on a stool, an ace bandage peeking from beneath the hem of her leggings. Ethan set a bowl of oatmeal in front of her with a flourish.

"Morning," he said, catching sight of Rowan and letting his shoulders ease. "Water's on for tea."

Tiffany looked up, cautious. "Morning, Mom."

Rowan kissed the top of her head, then set a hand on the wrap. "How's it feel?"

"Better," Tiffany said. "It only hurts if I point it wrong."

Guilt hit Rowan's ribs sharp as a stitch. Anger followed, a reflex she didn't analyze too closely. She straightened and poured tea with more force than necessary.

"It was my fault," Tiffany blurted, as if she'd been waiting for that exact sentence to find air before it dissolved. "Ms. Barlow said no high rocks. I went anyway because the list said chiton. I'm sorry."

No one should have to apologize for a child being a child. Rowan knew that. It didn't stop the tiny, bitter feeling pressing at the back of her throat. She hid it in her mug.

"No one's mad," she said, tone too flat to convince anyone. She took a breath and tried again. "We're okay. We'll rest it and try again later—on sand."

"I don't want you to be mad at Dad." Tiffany's eyes bounced between Rowan and Ethan.

Ethan moved behind her, hands hovering near the honey, then easing back. "It's on me," he said. "I could have kept her closer."

"It was an accident," Rowan said, a little too fast. The scalding scent of tea hit her nose. "We're all still learning how to do new things."

On the counter, Ethan's phone buzzed once. Twice. He didn't reach for it. The little rectangle pulsed anyway—out there tugging at him like a tide.

"They're still trying to resolve the contract?" She asked, eyeing the screen as if she could stare the messages quiet.

"I told them I'll call when I'm free," he said.

"You should have just gone," she said, and the words came out before she could pull them back. Petty. True. Both. "You could have avoided making everyone angry and gotten work done."

He blinked, and something shuttered. "I said I'd stay."

"Physically," she said, quieter.

He didn't answer that. He tipped honey into her mug with a steady hand he must have borrowed from yesterday, set it within reach, then reached for his laptop. She tasted the tea and didn't thank him.

"I have my follow-up with Dr. Cole today," she said, ears hot because it sounded like a challenge when it was a simple fact. "Kim is taking me."

"I can take you," he said. "I can build in a buffer around the call. It's fine."

"I don't want you to cram my life into your spare minutes," she said. "Kim's offered since the first day. It's taken care of."

Hurt flashed through his eyes so quickly that she might have imagined it. "Okay."

Tiffany's spoon clinked. She glanced between them as if she were trying to read a weather pattern. "We're still good, right?"

"We're good," Rowan said, too bright.

Ethan nodded. "We're good."

The doorbell chimed, then—the hollow thump of a package being abandoned on the welcome mat startled Fig.

"I've got it," Rowan said.

Ethan stepped in front of her before she'd taken a second step. "I'll grab it."

"I can walk to the door."

"I know." He lifted a palm, not touching her, but there all the same. "Why should you have to? You shouldn't be lifting heavy things."

"It's a box from the craft store," she said, voice going sharp because this was ridiculous and she had a ridiculous need to win. "It's not heavy."

"That's not the point."

"It's my door." She slid past him, heat pinging down her side where the movement pulled tight. The ache was enough to make her grit her teeth. She didn't change course.

"She's still angry." Tiffany tucked her chin and said to no one.

The box was small, weightless. Rowan picked it up with two fingers and shut the door with more care than she'd used opening it. She set the box on the table and waited for the rush of satisfaction. It didn't come. The ache did not just come from her abdomen.

Why couldn't she stop?

"I'm driving to drop-off," she announced, like a person with something to prove. "We can't keep pretending I'm an invalid."

Ethan's head came up. "You're not driving."

"I'm perfectly capable of—"

"Rowan." He kept the word quiet, like a stop sign with a palm in the middle. "Don't do that."

"Do what?"

"Turn this into a test." His jaw worked. "You don't have to pass anything to be allowed to be tired."

The worst part was the way her body agreed with him—soft at the knees, mind crowded by a weird fog that hadn't lifted since the hospital. It made her bristle harder.

"Give me the keys," she said.

"Not happening."

They stood there for a beat too long and said nothing. Then he held out his hand in a compromise he apparently decided on without telling her. "I'll drive. You can be in charge of the commentary."

"Lucky you," she said, and grabbed her bright red coat instead of the keys.

On the way down the stairs, the house felt too small. In the car, it felt like there wasn't enough air. The wipers squeaked across a windshield that didn't really need them.

"I'm not trying to box you out of your own life," he said finally, hands tight on the wheel. "I'm trying to take some weight you don't need to carry."

"If I let you do all of it now," she said, voice low, eyes on the rain-licked street, "What happens when you go back? What does that leave us?"

Ethan glanced at her and paused. He peered at Tiffany in the back seat. He knew they were worrying her, but it was better for her to see them trying and getting it wrong than not trying at all.

"We figure it out," he said. He reached out to place a hand on her leg while he was driving. "If we keep going like this, we're guaranteeing failure. We can't torch everything today because next week isn't solved."

"You already have one foot back in New York," she said, and the sound her heart made when she said it was an old one.

He flinched like she'd caught him doing something wrong. Then his face softened into something equal parts weary and raw. "I told them I couldn't be there."

"You told them 'not yet,'" she said.

He didn't answer that either.

At school, the morning crush had already begun—backpacks swinging, coffee cups flashing, children jolting like bees from half-stopped cars. Ethan pulled into the same spot he always did. He unbuckled to get out, then froze when Tiffany put a hand on his arm.

"I want to walk in by myself," she said, choosing each word like it had to be set in exactly the right place.

Rowan swallowed. "Baby, your ankle—"

"I'm okay." Tiffany squared her shoulders like she was slipping on a small suit of armor. "I want to try. Like a big kid."

Ethan glanced at Rowan.

Don't make it a fight.

Rowan wasn't sure whose voice said it louder—his or hers.

"Okay," she said, and found a smile that didn't quite feel like one. "Text when you're with Ms. Barlow."

Tiffany nodded, hoisted her backpack, leaned in to kiss each of their cheeks, then said, solemn as a benediction, "Be nice," before stepping out of the car.

When she looked back from the sidewalk, the look on her face was a new one—hope and test and a tiny flash of fear. Rowan lifted her hand. Tiffany lifted hers in return and disappeared into the flow.

"That stung," Rowan admitted to the windshield.

"It means we're doing something right," Ethan said. His voice wasn't quite steady.

"Or she's tired of our arguing," Rowan said.

He tilted his head. "That too."

The drive home was a series of small silences, punctuated by wiper squeaks and the heater's low hum. On the block before theirs, a pair of crows argued about something only crows could care about.

Kim's text arrived as Rowan was checking the mail slot. *Out front in five. I'm bringing you coffee.*

She lifted her keys and didn't look at Ethan as she slid them onto the dish. "Kim's here."

"I can still take you," he said. He didn't put his hand out this time. He had learned that much.

"I told her I'd be ready," she said, pulling on her coat. "Thank you for the tea."

He nodded. "I'll be here when you get home."

She wanted to say, "Good," and she wanted to say, "Go." The hot-cold conflict stayed in her throat and burned. Instead, she leaned in to kiss his cheek out of habit, or muscle memory, or something too new to be named, and walked outside.

Kim had her eyebrows up and two cups in the console when Rowan climbed into the passenger seat. "You look almost like yourself," she said. "Don't let that trick you into rearranging furniture."

Rowan laughed. "I'll try to restrain myself."

Chapter Twenty-Nine

Rowan

By the time they were back at the townhouse, Ethan's laptop had migrated to the kitchen table.

He crouched automatically to rescue a stray bead he'd found with his bare foot and flicked it into the small bowl Tiffany kept by the table. On his screen, a grid of faces waited—people who wanted something from him that had nothing to do with pendants boxed in velvet or girls in matching bracelets.

He gestured to the screen, pointed to his mic, and mouthed, "Sorry, I'll move soon." The furrow between his brows asked, *Everything okay?*

Rowan gave the smallest nod from the couch. For a minute, relief slipped in around the stiff parts inside her.

Then she noticed the box by the door. The way his chair hovered too close to the table. The faint echo of the ocean in her ribs—of the rock, the slip, the sound of Tiffany crying, and how quickly life could demand more than tea and scarves could fix.

Her phone buzzed. A client inquiry. A private commission.

She took the call at her worktable, shifting sketches until she felt like herself again—someone with a practice, a craft, a mind that made things. She pitched a piece with myrtle wood and soft stones and didn't say that the idea had been born on her couch, while the room smelled like tomatoes, and everyone had been laughing together.

When she hung up, Ethan was already closing his laptop, the practiced smile of a man who could sell a plan across time zones sliding off his face as he shut it.

"You want to go over your notes?" he asked, nodding at her sketchbook, careful and neutral.

"I've got it," she said lightly. "Thank you."

His mouth ticked. "Right."

She touched her stomach, forcing it to loosen. "I meant it. I'm okay."

"You're not wrong," he said. "And I'm not great at being told I'm not needed."

"I didn't say that," she said, then sighed because she had said exactly that without those exact words. "I...know you're leaving soon. I'm trying to make it not hurt."

"It doesn't work that way," he said, voice level, but his knuckles had gone white where his hand rested on the table. "Less now is not less later."

She stared at the crooked corner of the banner and wished she had something smarter to say. Instead, Rowan sat on the edge of the couch with her tea cupped between both hands.

From the kitchen came the quiet clink of Ethan emptying

the dishwasher, one plate at a time. *Giving her space, but staying close.*

Her phone lit up where it rested on the coffee table.

Bailey: *Call me. I have an idea.*

Rowan's pulse picked up in a way that had nothing to do with a fever. She glanced toward the kitchen. Ethan looked up and caught her eye.

"It's Bailey."

"Is everything okay?"

"I think so, she just said to call her."

"Okay," He tipped his chin toward the hallway. "I have some laundry to fold. Let me know if you need me."

Rowan nodded and watched him walk away before she pressed call and tucked her feet under her.

"Hey, Sugar," Bailey answered on the first ring, all Texas and steel. "How are my girls?"

"On the mend," Rowan said. "How's yours?"

"Bossy and charming, which means I'm raising her right." Bailey's tone softened. "You scared us. Are you doing better?"

"I am," Rowan said. "You said you wanted to talk?"

"Ah, right to the point. It's what I like about you." A quick rustle, then Bailey's no-nonsense voice. "Serenity is growing. Taylor and I are expanding A Stitch in Time into a cooperative focused on textiles, leatherwork, and jewelry. We want you to take the lead on the jewelry side. Not as a pop-in guest. As a partner. Design lead, featured line, meet-the-maker nights. We'll set you up with a studio space off Main St. Taylor will handle the pretty, I'll handle permits, you'll handle the pieces."

Rowan's fingers tightened around her mug. "Bailey."

"I'm not done," Bailey said, and Rowan could hear the smile. "We need a production brain who gets art and logistics. The co-op will include regional artists who haven't had a shot. You could mentor, set standards, teach them how to price their work without apologizing."

Rowan closed her eyes and pictured it: a bright room that smelled like cedar and metal and possibilities, clear drawers full of stones, a pegboard of tools, Tiffany curled at a worktable with a drawing pad, Rosie popping in for cupcake deliveries and opinions on ribbon.

"I'm listening," she said, low.

"Good." Bailey didn't pause. "There's more. Ladder H is reviving a small-batch distillery in Serenity. We've got the barrel house plans dusted and a site ready. It won't replace New York's marketing or production lines, but it will be real and matter. If you and Ethan are open to it, I want him to help me stand it up, then run it. Not as a visitor. As a presence."

Rowan blinked. "He—Bailey, he's on a track in Manhattan."

"He's also a dad who can build a life that fits his kids," Bailey said. It wasn't a handout. It was a hand held up. "I can take his brain and his numbers from anywhere. I'd rather have them from here...Rosie would, too."

"That's below the belt." Rowan looked around her townhouse and could feel how empty it was without the laughter of two little girls.

"I play to win."

A door clicked in the hall. Ethan appeared with a dish towel over his shoulder and stood where she could loop him in if she wanted to. Rowan put the call on speaker and filled him in.

"Bailey," Ethan said. "I'm not sure I'm following."

"I must have really caught you off guard, because I know you're better than that. Catch up," she said, amusement warming the words. "We're opening a co-op. We want Rowan as a partner. We're standing up a barrel house. We want you running it. We can pace it around kids' schedules and your current obligations. I know how to move mountains. So do you."

Ethan leaned against the archway, towel twisted in his hands, eyes steady on Rowan's face instead of the phone. "What would this mean for you right now?"

"For me," Bailey said, "it means I get to build with people I trust. For you two, it means you could stop dividing your lives between a thousand zip codes and choose one."

Taylor's voice chimed in faintly in the background, the warm glide of her California-meets-Texas drawl. "Tell her the name," she called.

Bailey sighed. "Taylor wants me to tell you we're calling the co-op, Stitch + Stone."

Rowan laughed, a quick, surprised sound that loosened something under her ribs. "A little from each of us. I like it."

"Think about it," Bailey said. "No pressure. Just...think." A beat passed. "I love you. Both of you. Kiss Tiff for me."

"We will," Rowan said, throat tight.

They hung up. The townhouse hummed around them, ordinary and full. Ethan crossed to the couch and set her tea back in her hands, then sat on the edge of the coffee table. "Rowan."

"I know," she said. "I'm breathing."

"Rosie snitched on us, didn't she?" he said.

"Sounds like it."

"Bailey has always been a fixer."

They stayed like that until her heart let go of its drumbeat. When she looked up, his expression was already honest. He wasn't braced for persuasion. He was waiting for the truth.

"Rosie misses Tiffany. Bailey knows you're struggling. I don't want to live with my life split in thirds," she said. "I don't want to keep being brave by myself. I don't want fear to keep pushing us apart. I want to make things that matter, teach girls like Rosie and Tiffany how to follow their passions, and come home to my family."

Something warm and wrecked moved over his face. He took a deep breath and set down his towel.

"I've been jealous," he said. "Watching how much time you and Bailey get with our girls. How much ease Jackson has with Sunday afternoons and school fairs. I've been clinging to a position in Manhattan because I convinced myself that success comes with a fancy address. I hate how much I've missed. I hate that I let it happen."

Rowan's chest ached in the best way. "Ethan."

He didn't look away. "I can carry the weight I need to carry from here. I can pitch a really small-batch program in Serenity. Not a vanity line. Real production, real tasting room, real jobs. We'll keep New York for what it's best at—marketing and flash. But we can make a home in Serenity, so we don't keep losing every time we get on a plane."

"And you won't resent me for asking you to do something...small?"

"This isn't small." His mouth tipped. "And, you aren't asking. I want this already. I needed a reason that wasn't rooted in fear. Bailey just handed me one. You and the girls handed me the rest."

She reached across the space between them, palm up. He took her hand and folded both of his around it, his thumb settling against the base of her fingers where he always went when he needed to steady them both.

"I'm scared," she said, because she refused to dress it up. "I've built my life on doing it myself. I know it's not the way you would do it."

Ethan looked at the floor, and then into Rowan's eyes. "I want to be the person who shows up for bean charts and library crafts and late-night tea. I want work to fit around that, not the other way around. I'm going to mess up. Stop me when I slide back into old habits."

"I will," she said. "And when I start doing everything again because I'm afraid to lean, tell me to sit down."

"Deal."

They sat in the quiet. Outside, rain had turned to a bright, thin sun, making the windowsill jars glow. A tender root had pushed from one lima bean, a white comma finding its line.

"Call Bailey back?" he asked, eyes still on her.

"In a minute," she said. She set her tea aside, slid closer on the couch, and linked both hands at the back of his neck. "Ethan," she said, a warning and an invitation.

"No heroics," he said. "I remember."

He kissed her anyway. Slow, certain, careful of the tender places. He tasted like honey and coffee and a week of learning how to be better. She answered with all the yeses she had and felt him sink into it. Heat sparked, held, and then settled into something stronger than rush—something that felt like an answer.

When they eased apart, cheeks flushed, breath even again, she pressed her forehead to his. "We're saying yes," she whispered.

"Yes," he said. "To being a family."

Chapter Thirty

Ethan

By lunchtime, Serenity's town square had found its Saturday rhythm—kids chasing bubbles by the gazebo, a vendor selling fried pickles, and the scent of sugar from Candy's bakery riding the warm Texas breeze.

Rowan stood in the doorway of the newly expanded shop and let herself take it all in. *Two Months.* They'd spent two months crafting their dream, and their grand opening was to-day.

Stitch + Stone gleamed. Whitewashed brick, brass rails, textiles on one side, shadowbox cases filled with jewelry on the other. Sunlight lay soft squares across herringbone floors and pooled in the glass boxes where her first official display sat front and center: barrel-wood beads smoothed to silk, smoky quartz, moonstone, petite hammered hoops catching the light, a bold piece grounded by charcoal oak—the card beneath read: *Bourbons & Bling, by Rowan Fontaine.*

"Stop pretending you're not going to cry," Taylor said, sliding in at her shoulder in wide-leg jeans and silver cuffs.

"I'm blaming your spotlights," Rowan said, knuckle to her eye.

"Good. The sign's straight. The glass is clean. People are already doing the little gasps."

The bell jingled. Tourists drifted in. An older couple paused at the case.

"Those beads are Ladder H barrel wood," Taylor told them, proud. "Local."

"Local," the woman repeated, squeezing her husband's arm.

The room filled with an energy that can't be manufactured. Bailey swept in with Rosie and a pink bakery box. "Candy sends her love," she said, hugging Rowan tight. "You did it."

"We did," Rowan said, meaning it.

Rosie pressed her nose to the glass. "Dad says your jewelry makes strong girls sparkle."

"Your dad knows things," Rowan said.

Jackson held the door for Molly. He took in the space, pleased with the work his crew had done. Molly glanced around with a pro's eye. "It's beautiful," she said, touching a lavender sachet from the textile side.

Jackson tapped the case. "I know that wood. There are a lot of old stories."

"Oak and strength," Rowan said.

Molly's mouth tipped. "Good tagline."

A man in a cap—one of the older locals who'd watched the Ladder H headlines too closely—wandered in, hands in his pockets. He gave Taylor a nod, then stopped at Rowan's case.

"That barrel bead work is something," he said. He pulled cash for a pair of hammered hoops. "Got a granddaughter. Hard to impress."

"Tell her that hoop is made to last," Rowan said, boxing the earrings with steady hands.

The bell rang again, and Ethan stepped in with Tiffany. The afternoon shifted with them. He'd already had a bit of Serenity in his bones, but now he was settling into it, letting the town claim him—sawdust flecks on his black T-shirt, the hard New York edge worn softer.

Tiffany beat him to the Rowan's case and planted both palms on the glass.

"The earrings are straight," she said. "I checked twice."

She glowed in her lemon-printed dress, with her teal-and-gold bracelet bright on her wrist.

"Hi, team," Ethan said, his gaze finding Rowan last and softening. He slipped an arm around her waist and kissed her temple. The room saw and did not look away.

An older woman—one who used to stare through him like he was only a headline—stepped forward and offered her hand. "Good to see you, Mr. Moore. We like folks who help build things here in Serenity."

"Yes, ma'am," he said, and meant more than manners.

Taylor lifted the bakery lid to reveal cupcakes crowned with buttercream roses. Tiffany stood beside her with a small chalkboard that read, "Patty Cakes by Candy." Free with purchase today.

People bought. Rosie worked the checkout as if she'd been born to it, handing out stickers to each customer.

Tiffany steered shy shoppers toward the 'Bourbons and Bling' case and said, in a stage voice that carried, "Those are real stones," like she was sharing classified information.

Near closing, with the store emptied of customers and kids, Ethan slid the lock with one hand, his other already finding Rowan's waist.

"Too tired for a walk while the lights come on?" he asked.

They stepped out into the warm Southern evening. Twinkling lights blinked awake across the square. A food truck still handed out paper cones of fries. Somewhere under the gazebo, a guitar strummed a low tune into the air.

Across the street in the park, Rosie and Tiffany darted back and forth, hands linked, dividing responsibilities with great seriousness: fries for Rosie, napkins for Tiffany.

Rowan glanced back at the glowing sign—Stitch + Stone.

Ethan brushed his thumb against her hip. "You okay?"

"I am," she said. "I'm happy."

"Me too." He leaned down, kissed her softly, then murmured, "Is it time?"

"Yes."

They followed the girls down the block toward the newly opened barrel house.

Edison bulbs zigzagged above the distillery patio, washing the long tables in warm light. Oak barrels stood like old sentries, their staves steeped in char and caramel. Behind the glass, the sign read 'Heartland Reserve.'

Investors spoke in low voices that loosened as tasting flights disappeared. Neighbors laughed. The air carried the scent of bourbon and Candy's pecan bars.

A man from the Ladder H board clapped Ethan's shoulder. "Heartland Reserve is outselling our traditional line."

"It's because it's good," Ethan said. "That's the heart of Ladder H."

The soft tap of Bailey's ring against her glass drew the patio to a hush.

"Tonight is a full-circle night," she said, no microphone needed. "Not just for our new friends and found family starting fresh in our humble little town, but we're bringing part of Ladder H back to Serenity. This goes beyond remembering our legacy, and becomes a promise to grow from it."

She let her gaze sweep across the tables.

"Today, we opened a home for artists who make this town shine. Stitch + Stone is crafting one-of-a-kind pieces from the barrels that make our whiskey the best. My mother would have loved this—rooted, generous, and a little fierce. We're here because people chose to show up for work, for each other, and for families made on purpose."

Glasses were lifted across the patio. Taylor and Clinton raised theirs. Jackson and Molly followed, shoulder to shoulder.

"Oh, it's the perfect happy ending," Candy gushed, pressing a tissue to her eyes as her husband, Lincoln, slipped an arm around her waist.

When the small crowd at Rowan's jewelry display near the bar thinned, Ethan tipped his head toward the porch.

She set her glass into Taylor's waiting hands and followed him.

From the rail, the string of lights looked like someone had scattered stars across the town square as the last light of day faded. Rowan's pendant—a small, hammered disc threaded with a barrel bead—rested warm against her skin.

"Ever think we'd land here?" he asked.

"No," she said, honest and sure. "But I like that we both got lost in the same direction."

He thumbed the pendant, then let his hand fall until the bead touched her collarbone. "Bourbons & Bling," she said. "Bringing us together."

"I moved part of the company halfway across the country to stand beside you," he said.

"Then it's official," she said. "We're building a legacy for each other."

"I love you," he said.

"I love you, too." She returned and kissed him slowly.

Back on the lawn, the girls had claimed a picnic blanket near the edge of the glow. Tiffany sprawled close to Rosie, and they'd built a small picnic from the party's charcuterie board, knees touching, hands colliding as they reached for bits of meat, cheese, crackers, and grapes.

Rowan slid her hand into his. Skin to skin, easy.

"I think this is the life I was always trying to build," he said.

"Good," she said. "Let's keep building it."

He looked out at tables and round barrel windows. Heartland Reserve glowed through the glass.

"Come on," Rowan said, shoulder to his. A quiet nudge. "We have people to thank, and work in the morning."

Epilogue

Ethan & Rowan

The auditorium at Serenity Elementary hummed with nerves and whispers. Programs rustled. Phone screens glowed as parents staked out aisles for the best line-of-sight shots. Somewhere backstage, a kazoo started by accident. The music teacher put a hand to her forehead and shrugged, long-suffering and unsurprised.

Rowan slid into the middle of the fourth row and let the noise wash over her. The seats were close, the air a little warm, the stage curtain a deep purple that had seen years of pageants and talent shows. It all felt right. She smoothed the program in her lap and tucked the stack of tissues into her bag—she told herself they were for other people.

All of their friends filled the row.

Jackson took the aisle and gave up his elbow room without complaint when his wife, Molly, arrived with a bottle of water and a bag of peppermints that had probably come from her glove box. Candy slipped in with a contraband bakery box balanced on one palm, pressed it into Bailey's hands, and hissed, "For later." Lincoln followed, folding his long frame into the narrow seat and leaning in to kiss Candy's temple. Mac, Bailey's husband, with his tie off and sleeves rolled up, claimed the end of the row beside her, then reached past her to squeeze Rowan's shoulder.

"I'm proud of you," he said.

Taylor and Clinton took the two seats behind them. Taylor's cuffs flashed when she waved. Clinton's hand found her knee, thumb drawing an idle line. Rowan suspected Taylor pretended not to notice.

Ethan dropped into the seat beside Rowan with two paper cups of auditorium coffee and the look of a man who had counted three routes to the bathroom and chosen the one with the longest distance to avoid the chaos. He set one cup in her hand and kept the other, shoulder pressed to hers.

"You made it," she said, smiling into the rim.

"Wouldn't miss it," he said, low enough for only her to hear. He nodded toward the stage. "Backstage report says our star is calm. Her sister has opinions on blocking."

"Of course she does."

He laughed, then glanced at the program in case the girls quizzed him later. "How many songs can they fit into a forty-minute play?"

"More than the legal limit," Jackson whispered across to Molly without shame.

"Shh," Molly warned, her mouth curving.

The house lights dimmed. A hush rippled through the room, soft and expectant. The curtain jerked once, then lifted to reveal a cardboard skyline taped to the back wall and an entire herd of second- and third-graders dressed as seasons, animals, and at least one enthusiastic traffic cone.

Rowan's heart found her throat. Tiffany and Rosie stepped into the wash of light from opposite wings, robes swishing, hair smoothed within an inch of its life. Their bracelets caught the stage lights, teal and gold, bright against small wrists. Rosie's crown leaned to one side. Tiffany straightened her shoulders the exact way she did before walking into school, chin tipped, eyes scanning until she found her anchors.

"Ethan," Rowan breathed.

"I see them," Ethan said, already on his feet for the first applause.

Tiffany located their row and grew two inches. Rosie grinned like she owned the building. The music started, and the kazoo mercifully absent this time, but fifty small voices launched into a song about trying again.

By the second chorus, Rowan had forgotten to breathe. She watched the girls move in step with their class and with each other. Rosie took one tiny half-step back to give Tiffany room. Tiffany lifted her hand at the exact moment the teacher had taught them, then squeezed her eyes shut on the high note, and hit it perfectly.

"Look at her," Bailey murmured, tissue already in hand. Mac passed her another without comment.

Candy sniffed into her sleeve. "I didn't think I'd cry until the end."

"You always cry at the beginning," Lincoln said, amused and tender.

On stage, Tiffany delivered her line in a voice that carried all the way to the rafters. "We did it together," she declared, clear as a bell.

Rosie bumped her shoulder and whispered something that made Tiffany's mouth curve. Neither girl missed their mark.

Ethan's hand found Rowan's under the shared armrest. Their fingers threaded together, a familiar shape now. She looked down at their hands, then back up at the stage, and felt the parts of her life overlay: the girl in the lemon dress who had learned not to hide, the woman with her name on a glass case, the man who had learned to stay. It fit.

When the final number swelled, the audience rose as one. Programs became fans. Phones lifted toward the ceiling, flashes popping. The music teacher bowed her head, clearly glad it would be another year before the next show.

The curtain bobbed, but didn't fully close.

The cast lined up in two crooked rows and bowed. Tiffany and Rosie clasped hands in the center. Tiffany spotted Ethan and lifted their joined hands high.

"Look, Dad!" she called, bright and unafraid. "We did it!"

"You sure did, sweetheart," he called back, voice steady, pride warming the three words. The man in the row behind them clapped him on the back as if he'd won a prize.

The lights came up hard. People blinked and stretched. Someone lost a shoe and found it two rows away. The buzz doubled, loud and happy, as families spilled into the aisles.

"Here they come," Jackson said, leaning back to let a parade of grandparents shuffle by.

Rosie and Tiffany dodged three hugs from classmates and

a near collision with a cardboard tree, arriving at their row with momentum. Tiffany barreled into Rowan first, careful even in her excitement.

Rowan kissed her cheek and breathed in the school auditorium, the glitter glue, and the fruit snacks. Rosie leaned into Ethan's side like a bolt hitting home.

"How did we do?" Tiffany asked, breathless.

"Perfect," Rowan said.

"High praise," Rosie said, but the words couldn't hide her grin.

"Your duet was spot on," Molly added. "I clocked your half step."

Rosie lit up. Jackson raised both hands like a referee signaling a good call, then bent to hand over Molly's peppermints.

"Ms. Taylor," Tiffany said, turning with sudden gravity, "did you see how we did the costume change? Very professional."

"I did," Taylor said, delighted. "You have a future in quick change. I'm hiring you both for five dollars a show."

"Ten," Rosie said, instantly. Clinton choked on his coffee and passed her an approving nod.

Candy produced the contraband cupcakes. "Just a taste," she said, passing the box down the row. "Don't tell the janitor. He's still upset about that time in grade school when I accidentally started that food fight."

"Accidentally?" Bailey laughed. "That man knows everything."

"You two are going to be impossible to live with," Mac told the girls, eyes bright. "You were the best thing on that stage."

"We know," Rosie said, then winced, correcting herself. "I mean, thank you."

Lincoln lifted an eyebrow at Candy. "Where did she learn that?"

"From me," Candy said, unrepentant.

Ethan watched all of them: the noise and the sugar and the scolding and the affection. He bent to adjust Tiffany's crown. She tilted her face up to him and smiled, glowing like a star.

When they finally made it to the aisle, the crowd tugged them toward the doors and into the cool night. A PTA member had strung a few hasty strands of lights in the parking lot with access to a ladder and no fear.

They paused on the sidewalk, not ready to split. Traffic cones protected the crosswalk, though Rosie shifted them two inches to the left for reasons known only to Rosie. Tiffany leaned into Rowan's side and hummed the final song's last bars under her breath.

"Next week," Ethan said, his voice low enough that it wrapped warm around Rowan more than anyone else, "I've got a short trip to New York. Three days. Then I'm back. The rest of the month is here."

"Good," Rowan said. "I have co-op orders piling up and a new apprentice starting. I'll need your logistics brain."

Ethan made a show of considering. "You sure you trust me with the bead inventory?"

"Not even a little," she said, and his grin landed like home.

Bailey and Mac gathered their things for the drive to the ranch. Candy and Lincoln promised to swing by Stitch + Stone early with a delivery.

"Group hug," Rosie announced, then executed it herself, flinging away dignity to wrap her arms around whoever was within her reach. It turned into a cheerful knot of friends and elbows.

They separated in a jumble of goodbyes. The girls ran ahead, stopping at the edge of the curb, hands clasped. Their bracelets flashed once more under the parking lot lights.

Rowan laced her fingers through Ethan's and didn't let go. "I'm happy," she said.

He looked down at her, then across the street at the school with its clean brick and hand-lettered banners, and thought of the beans on the windowsill and of the way Tiffany had lifted her hand high and claimed the moment with all her heart. "Me too."

They crossed, a little island of three, then four as Rosie reached back without looking and found Ethan's sleeve, tugging him closer as if she knew exactly which direction they were headed.

Behind them, the auditorium doors swung open and shut, sending out a last wave of sound. Ahead, the town of Serenity settled in for the night.

"Let's go," Ethan said.

They both knew they were heading toward a promise, and they were finally making what they'd both come to want more than anything...a home.

"Together," Rowan said.

About Amber W. Lynne

An award-winning author from the misty, coffee-scented landscapes of the Pacific Northwest, Amber blends slow-burn tension, heart-tugging emotion, and just the right amount of sweet and heat into every story she writes. The relationships are relatable and her heroines are fierce, independent, and (sometimes) a little stubborn, but they always find the right man to love them.

Fueled by caffeine and an unshakable belief in love, Amber has been crafting stories since childhood, drawn to the way romance can heal, challenge, and transform. When she's not writing, she's playing with her five kids (I KNOW!), helping fellow writers embrace their literary dreams, or spending time with her hubby making a love story of her own.

<u>Ways to stay in touch:</u>

- Subscribe to her Newsletter

- Via email: info@AmberWLynne.com

- Follow on Instagram - AmberLynne.Author

- Follow on Facebook - Amber W. Lynne, Author

Also by Amber W. Lynne

<u>Working For Love</u>

Lanyards & Lariats
Toolbelts & Ties
Spreadsheets & Sprinkles
Gowns & Gavels
Bourbons & Bling
Holly & Heartbeats

Leave a review at your favorite retailer, and sign-up for Amber's newsletter, to get more love stories, sneak peeks, a chance at Beta or ARC reads, and exclusive giveaways.

To find more books by Amber W. Lynne, visit:
https://amberlynneauthor.com

Holly & Heartbeats

Working for Love, Book 6

Visit https://AmberLynneAuthor.com and subscribe to our monthly newsletter to receive launch updates, sneak peeks, exclusive giveaways, and early access to beta and ARC reads!

A tub of mint chip sat like a quiet accomplice on the counter, sweating under the kitchen lights. Jess knew—without pretense or illusion—that eating straight from the container in her softest pajamas didn't count as celebrating. Especially not at Christmas time.

Her clinic was closed for the holidays. She had no idea what to do with herself, but she couldn't ask her staff to keep working just because she didn't know how to take a break. The spoon bumped against the carton as she scooped aimlessly; her laptop was nearby with half a dozen open tabs about charity gift drives, rerun holiday rom-coms, and a too-earnest article titled, Ten

Ways to Love Being Alone Over the Holidays.

None of it appealed.

The living room was quiet; with only the soft glow of the twinkling lights she had set on a timer. She hadn't bothered putting up a tree, just the lights and a cinnamon-scented candle burning out of habit. Her cozy bungalow in Serenity didn't feel as warm when every room echoed more than usual, and she had nowhere else to go but to the next room.

Her phone buzzed once on the table.

She didn't need to look. She already knew.

Jackson.

A text. Then a call.

Jess let it ring twice, then picked it up with practiced ease. "Hey."

Still pretending that building your own gingerbread clinic out of graham crackers and 'Sarcasm counts as self-care?' Jackson's warm, familiar voice came through with a lopsided grin. She didn't need to see to hear.

Jess leaned back against the counter and let her eyes close for half a second. "If that were true, I'd be certified by the American Board of Baked Architecture by now. No gingerbread tonight, though. Just...freezer aisle therapy."

There was a pause filled with background noise, Molly probably laughing softly in the distance.

Jess softened. "How's she feeling? Still holding that baby hostage?"

"Yep," Jackson exhaled. "Due any day now. She's trying to decide if the baby needs antlers on its hospital cap."

Jess laughed, then bit down on it, warmth swelling and

tugging something low in her chest. "Sounds like her."

There was another thoughtful pause before Jackson added, "You sure you're okay spending the holiday alone?"

She could hear the frown in his voice. That old protectiveness she used to lean into without thinking. He knew the only family she had was a found one, and that, without her friends, she'd be alone.

"I'm good, Jackson. Seriously."

"I just..." he trailed off, then shifted. "You've been there for me every Christmas since—well, since a decade ago. I know we aren't 'us' anymore, but we've kinda had a tradition."

She glanced at the condensation pooling beneath her untouched ice cream.

A breath hitched in her chest—unbidden—and suddenly she was back in her old kitchen, three Christmases ago.

Jackson had burned the crescent rolls *again*. The timer was ignored as she danced around the tile, Bing Crosby crooning from his speaker. She'd been half-dressed for a shift at the clinic, laughing as he spun her under the garland strung above the cabinets. Her pager buzzed—two sharp jolts against her hip—and everything froze.

"Don't," he'd said, catching her hand before she could reach for it. "You promised. Just this morning."

She hesitated—just a second. But her career always came first, didn't it? Patients didn't care that she'd stayed up until the wee hours hanging ornaments or that the stuffing was still cold in the middle. There was a flu outbreak. A pregnant teenager in her third trimester. No coverage.

Jess had kissed him on the cheek, grabbed her keys, and

whispered, "I'll only be gone an hour."

He smiled, soft and tired. "You said that last time."

She hadn't made it back until well after dark.

The holiday rolls ended up in the trash, along with the tinsel he'd tried to hang on the mantle. That night, he curled up with the leftover ham she barely touched and watched Miracle on 34th Street alone before falling asleep on the couch.

She remembered standing in the hallway, coat still on, watching his shoulders from behind and thinking, *this isn't what either of us asked for.*

And that was their problem. She hadn't offered him the same commitment Molly had...Jess hadn't given him a family.

Now, the candle on her counter flickered, and the cheap wick sputtered.

Jess pulled the ice cream closer and took a slow, steady bite, the mint sharp on her tongue. They no longer celebrate that version of Christmas.

Not anymore.

"We did." Jess let the truth settle on her tongue, steady but kind. She'd grown and taken a few lessons from him, too. "But this year is different. You and Molly are starting something new."

"That doesn't mean we can't still—"

"It means I want you to have this fully," she said gently. "The waiting. The chaos. The antler caps. All of it."

Jackson went quiet. When he spoke again, it was softer. "And what are you going to do, Doc?"

There it was.

Jess swallowed the hollow ache forming behind her ribs. "A

date with a blanket, a movie about improbable holiday miracles, and possibly the worst whipped topping known to mankind." Her smile never quite reached her voice. "Don't worry about me."

We'll do better next year. We'll find other traditions...when things aren't so new.' She could hear him sigh softly through his nose.

"We always do." Molly scooped out some softened ice cream from the carton. "I've got to get back to my creamed ice before it melts."

"Alright," said Jackson, resigned.

"Tell Molly I said she's got this."

"She's got this," Jackson agreed. "And Jess, seriously. If you change your mind—"

"I won't."

He didn't push further. That was the difference now—he knew when to let her go.

When the call ended, she set her phone down next to the carton and gazed at the laptop. The blinking cursor waited on the half-read article. She closed the tab without reading another word.

Carrying the carton and laptop, Jess moved into the living room and settled onto the couch, her legs curled underneath her. The remote was across the room, deliberately out of reach—a self-imposed test of willpower from earlier that now just felt more like an inconvenience.

No voices. No music. No clatter of baking. Even the candle's flickering flame felt underwhelming.

The silence wasn't solitude anymore.

It was hollowness. It was the absence of anything that mattered or brought a semblance of holiday cheer.

She'd done holidays alone before. Even last year, she'd shown up at Jackson and Molly's with a ham and hung a few ornaments on their tree. But this? This year, they didn't need her. Which was good. Progress. Everyone deserved that joy.

What she hadn't realized—what now lived in her doubt—was how much of her holiday spirit had always been borrowed from others' moments. She'd never actually created her own. She rubbed her wrist absently with her thumb—the calming trick she used between patient triage and 2 a.m. newborn check-ins.

Pulling the laptop to her knees, she clicked open a new tab without thinking and typed: *Christmas retreats near me.*

Enter.

A cascade of links loaded with spa weekends, yoga getaways, and silence lodges.

But just above the scrolling list was one small photo. A cedar-shingled house strung with white lights. A wreath on a fence. *The Holly House Inn.*

The site was simple. It featured a few photos of an old wooden porch and a fire-lit parlor, but no big-city branding. Just soft light, pine boughs, and a kitchen that looked like a dozen generations of grandmothers had baked holiday treats there.

The tagline made something soft unravel for her.

Wrapped in tradition, with the promise of home.

It was simple. Honest. Jess had built her life on reliability—on steady plans, clean breakrooms, and framing patient charts like puzzles she was trained to fix. She had spent years helping others while quietly setting aside her own wants.

Truth was, she didn't know what her own traditions looked like.

The ones she'd grown up with had faded after college, and the ones with Jackson...those belonged to someone else now. Someone who wore fuzzy socks on Christmas morning and belly-laughed through burned biscuits in a home bursting with future.

This. The site promised something gently impossible for someone like her: a holiday without pretending. A space that was already warm. A quiet place to miss no one and nothing, because it wouldn't expect her to carry the entire holiday season alone. She could enjoy the holiday without a plan preset by someone else.

It had been a long time since a holiday week had sounded like a gift instead of a task.

She re-read the tagline once more, slower this time.

Wrapped in tradition, with the warmth of home.

And for reasons she couldn't name, her throat tightened.

Jess didn't give herself time to hesitate.

Click. Reserve.

She barely acknowledged the confirmation before gently closing her laptop and gazing into the steady flicker of her candle.

She wasn't running away from the solitude of her little home. Not exactly. She'd find new traditions at The Holly House Inn, and maybe, for a change, make a few of her own.

AVAILABLE AT MAJOR BOOK RETAILERS